Angel sent th
the space bet
satisfaction when his gaze met hers, and he
faltered over his words.

His eyes were extraordinary—an intriguing
shade that hovered between gray and green.
Occasionally when he hit a favorite topic, his
eyes would glow and the green would turn to
a bright emerald.

Abandoning her notepad, Angel rested her
chin against her palm and studied the young
history teacher. He was as blond as she was
dark. Tall and muscular, he always dressed
professionally. Today he'd worn her favorite
combination, a denim shirt and khaki pants.
He looked, she thought idly, just like she liked
her men to look.

Immediately the sheer absurdity of the thought
struck her and she laughed out loud.

"Angel, perhaps you'd like to share with
the class what you find so amusing about
nerve gas usage during the Vietnam War."
Jake Weston quirked his eyebrow.

Angel groaned to herself. Even though she was
twenty-six and not eighteen years old, she still
refused to look foolish. Angel thought quickly.
"That they had the *nerve* to use it?"

Laughter filled the classroom. Jake Weston's
lips twitched, but his expression was stern.

Books by Cynthia Rutledge

Love Inspired

Unforgettable Faith #102
Undercover Angel #123

CYNTHIA RUTLEDGE

lives in the Midwest and has enjoyed reading romance since her teens. She loves the fact that you can always count on a happy ending.

Writing inspirational romance has been especially gratifying because it allows her to combine her faith in God with her love of romance.

Undercover Angel is her second book for Love Inspired.

Undercover Angel
Cynthia Rutledge

Published by Steeple Hill Books™

STEEPLE HILL BOOKS

Steeple
Hill™

ISBN 0-373-87129-5

UNDERCOVER ANGEL

Copyright © 2000 by Cynthia Rutledge

This edition published by arrangement with Steeple Hill Books.

Visit us at www.steeplehill.com

Printed in U.S.A.

And be ye kind one to another, tenderhearted, forgiving one another, even as God for Christ's sake hath forgiven you.

—*Ephesians* 4:32

To my daughter Wendy
The light of my life

Chapter One

Angel Morelli chewed on her yellow number-two pencil and paid rapt attention to the man at the front of the room.

You have beautiful eyes.

She offered up the compliment, sending it silently across the space between them, smiling with satisfaction when his gaze met hers and he faltered over his words.

His eyes *were* extraordinary—an intriguing shade that hovered between gray and green. Occasionally when he hit a favorite topic, his eyes would glow and the green would turn to a bright emerald. But now, at the end of the day, they'd dulled to a lifeless putty color.

Abandoning her notepad, Angel rested her chin

against her palm and studied the young history teacher. He was as blond as she was dark. Tall and muscular, he always dressed professionally. Today he'd worn her favorite combination: a denim shirt and khaki pants. A brightly colored cartoon tie hung loosely around his neck, secured with a once-crisp knot. He looked, she thought idly, just like she liked her men to look.

Immediately the sheer absurdity of the thought struck her and she laughed out loud.

"Angel, perhaps you'd like to share with the class what you find so amusing about nerve gas usage during the Vietnam War." Jake Weston quirked his eyebrow questioningly.

She groaned to herself. Even though she was twenty-six and not eighteen, she still refused to look foolish in the suddenly sharp and assessing eyes of what were supposed to be her peers. Angel thought quickly. "That they had the *nerve* to use it?"

Laughter filled the classroom. She stifled an impulse to smile and instead smirked.

The teacher's lips twitched but his expression was stern. "That will—"

A bell rang and the sounds of conversation and chairs scraping the floor drowned out his words. He halted, as if knowing it would be futile to talk above the clatter that accompanied the end of each school day.

Angel quickly shoved her books into her backpack. She'd promised to meet Crow at three-thirty, and if she hurried she'd have just enough time to grab a candy bar.

Shrugging on her leather jacket, she made her way down the crowded aisle, her thoughts already jumping ahead to her rendezvous in the park.

"Not so fast, Angel." A familiar deep voice stopped her just before she reached the door. "I need you to stick around for a few minutes. We need to talk."

She turned slowly and tried to hide her irritation. Normally she'd give anything to spend some time with Jake Weston, but today her meeting with Crow took priority. "I'm in kind of a hurry."

"This won't take long."

"Yeah, right."

"Five minutes max." He flashed her an engaging smile. "Guaranteed."

Angel heaved a resigned sigh. The super-size Milky Way would have to wait. Goodness knows, Crow wouldn't.

She flipped her hair back from her face and swaggered to the front of the room, not an easy task when your fashionably clunky shoes weighed a ton and your baggy jeans threatened to dip lower with each step.

With each step, his classically handsome features grew more pronounced. With each step, her heart rate increased and the hungry growl in her stomach no longer mattered.

"I knew you couldn't resist me forever." Her flippant words ran far too close to the truth to be a joke, yet a boy heading out the door snickered.

Jake shot him a quelling glance before his gaze shifted to the last of the students exiting the room. "Marylou, will you leave the door open as you leave?"

"Sure, Mr. Weston." The plump blonde gave him an adoring look.

Angel stifled a groan. She hoped she'd never been that obvious when she'd been a senior.

Jake Weston's gaze shifted to the stack of papers on his desk and he gestured to a nearby chair. "Have a seat."

Angel ignored the offer. Instead she braced a hand against the side of his heavy wooden desk and leaned over the cluttered surface. She inhaled the spicy scent of his cologne and waited for him to look up.

After what seemed an eternity, his gaze rose. "Angel—"

Their eyes locked. Their breathing came in unison. Her legs turned to jelly. Never in all her twenty-six years had she felt more like a school-girl.

She ignored the unfamiliar butterflies and flashed him her most engaging smile. "Are you sure we should be meeting like this?"

A startled expression crossed his face.

He laughed finally, a self-deprecating grin twisting his mouth. "You really had me going. Believe it or not, for a second I thought you were serious."

Angel shrugged, her smile lingering an instant longer. She shoved the hard wood chair against the wall and slowly sat down, using the time to regain her composure.

Although she was pleased he hadn't responded to her bait, a tiny part of her couldn't help but wish he had. It had been a long time since she'd flirted with any man, much less one this handsome, and she found herself reluctant to end the game so quickly. She batted her heavily mascaraed lashes. "Are you sure I was kidding?"

Though she'd meant the words to come out light and teasing, the natural huskiness of her voice added a decidedly sensual edge.

A hint of unease clouded his gaze, and he sat back in his chair putting distance between them. Angel cursed her reckless impulsiveness.

"I'm just foolin' with ya." She flashed a smile

and punched his shoulder. "I'm not trying to get it on. I've already got an old man."

The tension in his expression eased. "You've already got an old man?"

"Yep." She blew a bubble, then popped it with her finger. "He's old, but not as old as you."

Angel caught a hint of unmistakable relief in the teacher's eyes before he grabbed his planner from the desk drawer. "I know you're in a hurry so I'll get to the point. You've been a student here at Woodland Hills for what—two weeks?"

"Something like that," she said.

It had actually been closer to three. Three frustrating weeks of listening and asking and observing. Three weeks gone—and she knew nothing more than when she'd first arrived.

She shifted her gaze from his face, settling on the clock over his left shoulder. Three-fifteen.

"I don't know if you've heard, but last night Mr. Harper was in a car accident. He's going to be okay but he won't be back this semester."

"And that has what to do with me?" Angel had briefly met the rotund and balding guidance counselor when she'd enrolled. She hadn't seen him since. The man had been pleasant but disorganized. She pushed the memory aside of how he'd messed up her schedule, offered up a prayer for his recovery, and quickly calculated how long it would take her to reach the park.

"Well..." Jake cleared his throat.

She shifted impatiently.

"One of Mr. Harper's primary duties was to help students who..." He hesitated again.

She glanced at the clock and groaned. At this rate she'd never make it to the park on time. "Go ahead. Just say it. Harper was in charge of the losers."

Jake's eyes widened and he jerked back as if she'd struck a physical blow.

"Okay, I can tell you're into all that PC garbage. Let me rephrase." She sighed and recited the line in a singsong manner. "Mr. Harper worked with those of us labeled 'at-risk.'"

Angel could allude to her bottom-feeding status in Woodland Hills's food chain without a twinge of angst. Being out of high school eight years had taught her there was more to life than being Homecoming Queen or a cheerleader. But she was not so far removed that she didn't realize that if she really were a high school student in this situation, she would appreciate the teacher's sensitivity.

Jake's neck turned red above his collar. "Angel, please don't misunderstand—"

"Don't worry about it." She snapped her gum.

"I have high self-esteem. I can handle it. I know I'm a person with a lot of potential."

"Yes, you are." His words were sincere and reassuring. He'd totally missed her sarcasm. "If you just apply yourself, there's no limit to how far you can go."

"Yeah, you're right. My answer about the nerve gas *was* brilliant."

She checked the clock again and her heart shifted into high gear. If she ran most of the way, she might still be on time. She stood. "I hate to cut this party short, but I'm a busy girl. I've got places to go, people to see."

"Okay." He held up a hand. "Short and sweet. I need to set up a time for a home visit. Mr. H had gotten all but yours done."

"Home visit?" She forced herself to remain calm. After all, he had to be kidding. Didn't he? She cast a surreptitious glance, searching for a sign that he was just teasing—a twinkle in his eye, a twitch of his lip, even a raised brow. But all she found was an earnest expression. Her heart sank.

"It's not as bad as it sounds." His dimples flashed unexpectedly. "It gives me a chance to meet your parents."

After more than ten years, the response was automatic. "They're dead."

"I'm sorry to hear that." Concern darkened his gaze.

"Yeah, well, me too."

"You live with relatives?"

She shook her head. "Been there. Done that."

"Group home?"

Angel lied with a straight face. "About as bad. Foster parents."

He leaned back in his chair and steepled his fingers beneath his chin. "Do you like them?"

She gave him a pitying glance. "What do you think?"

"I have no idea."

The last foster home she'd been in, the one she'd left the day she turned eighteen, flashed in her mind.

"They're old and crabby, and the place stinks like Ben-Gay," she said flatly.

"That's too bad." Jake shifted in his chair and shuffled a gray mechanical pencil from one hand to another. He paused, then cleared his throat. "How about I come by tonight after dinner? Say, about six?"

"Make it tomorrow. I'm busy tonight." Angel didn't wait for his reply. She slung her bag over her shoulder and headed for the door.

"Six o'clock?" he called to her.

"Sounds good." Angel turned in the doorway. "Just don't say I didn't warn you about the smell."

She hurried down the shiny linoleum, her mind racing as fast as her steps. He'd caught her off guard with his request and she'd thought fast. Maybe a little too fast. Still, how hard could it be to come up with a couple of old, crabby, foster parents?

Jake stuck his head into the principal's office. "You needed to see me, Tom?"

Tom Jorgens looked up and nodded for him to come in. In his late forties, Tom had more the air of a Fortune 500 CEO than a midwestern high school principal. His dark brown hair was cut short in the latest style, his suit was hand tailored, and his cuff links were real diamonds. The tortoiseshell reading glasses he'd recently acquired completed the picture.

Jake was already in the room by the time he realized Tom was on the phone. Trying to be as quiet as possible, he walked across the thick plush carpet and took a seat in his favorite leather wingback. His gaze shifted slowly around the room. After almost three years, he still marveled at the magic Tom's wife had wrought with her decorating skill. Done in burgundy and blues, the once-sterile office now radiated the rich warmth usually seen only in the offices of top administrators.

The school district's money for renovation had been nonexistent, but Jane Jorgens had declared the redone office to be her twenty-fifth wedding anniversary gift to her husband. She'd died less than a year later. Sadness rose inside Jake, despite his efforts to squelch it.

Jane's unexpected death in a car accident had hit Tom hard. His despair had been so immense, so profound that the staff had wondered if he would survive.

Tom hung up the phone and smiled. The simple gesture emphasized his gauntness. Never a small man, he'd lost so much weight over the past year that his clothes practically hung on his skeletal frame. Jake wondered if Tom would ever get over his grief.

"So, have you heard any more from the cops?" Tom snapped.

Jake didn't even blink. Tom had become notorious for his abrupt manner; it was as much a change as his physical appearance. Still, Jake, of all people, could understand. He'd lost his brother last year and he knew *he'd* certainly changed. The part of Jake that had been trusting and filled with God's spirit had died in that apartment with Jim, and had not been resurrected.

"Well, have you?" Tom's smile faded and his gaze sharpened. Lately, all Tom could talk about was the fact that a police investigation into an interstate methamphetamine ring seemed to point to someone at the school.

"Why would they contact me and not you?" Jake forced himself to ignore the impatience in the principal's voice. Once jovial and even-tempered, the principal had become irritable, lashing out at staff over trivial matters he wouldn't previously have given a second thought. They'd all learned to walk on eggshells.

Even now, Jake chose his words carefully. "I haven't spoken to anyone connected with the investigation in almost two months—not since before Christmas."

"You don't think they'd plant another undercover officer here without letting us know?"

"I can't imagine why they'd do that," Jake said thoughtfully. "They let us know when they'd placed the other two."

"I think they blame us." Tom's eyes glittered, and he leaned forward resting his elbows on the desk. "They think we blew the cover on those other two."

"C'mon Tom. Only you, Bob Harper and I knew they were undercover," Jake said. "And we both know Bob didn't say a word."

"What about those new students this semester?" Like a bulldog, Tom refused to let the subject drop. "Any chance one of them could be a cop?"

"No," Jake said immediately. "Not a one."

"Don't speak so quickly." Tom tapped his pen like a drumstick against the dark cherry wood desktop. "Give it some thought. How many of them are there?"

Jake thought for a moment. "Three. Two girls and one boy."

"Anything suspicious about any of them?"

"You mean like have I caught them handcuffing other students to the flagpole? Or reading someone their Miranda rights?"

Tom shot him a look that said his attempt at humor wasn't appreciated.

Jake wiped away his smile and forced a suitably serious expression. He thought for a moment about the new students: Emily, Angel and Kirk.

Of the three, the only one that had made any sort of impact was Angel. With her wild dark hair tumbling past her shoulders and her sexy swagger, he was ashamed to admit, she'd captured his attention. But obviously she was too blatant, too in-his-face to be an undercover cop.

"Well?" Tom's gaze was sharp and probing, and it was all Jake could do not to redden.

"Nope." Jake shook his head. "Not an undercover cop in the group."

The pen ceased its tapping, and Tom's sudden sigh of relief caught Jake off guard.

"I can't tell you how happy that makes me," Tom said.

"What does it matter?" Surprise made Jake speak freely. "The others didn't cause any problem."

"You're right," Tom said. "I just like to know who is in my school. If you hear anything..."

The principal's sentiment made perfect sense. His ultimate responsibility was to the students, and it certainly wasn't too much for a principal to expect to be informed if he had cops posing as students in his school.

"You can count on me," Jake said without hesitation. "If I get even the slightest hint someone's not who they appear to be, you'll be the first one I'll call."

Chapter Two

Angel spotted Crow instantly. She couldn't believe a man who'd just turned thirty-two years old could look like he was twenty-five. He sat on a bench beneath a huge sycamore, using the tree as a backrest. With eyes narrowed to block the sun, he gave the appearance of being half asleep. But Angel knew he missed nothing. Not the way the mothers gathered their little ones when they ventured into the leafy shade, not the curious glances of the elderly walkers circling the park and not Angel's approach from the south.

She slid down the bench feeling ridiculously small and fragile next to his bulk.

He didn't utter a single word but she could tell her lateness had put him off. Salvador Tucci was not a man to cross. Friends had nicknamed him Crow because of his shoulder-length hair and black belt in karate. Eyes that glittered with a savage intensity and a barbed wire tattoo encircling a muscular bicep only added to his menacing appearance.

"You're late." He scowled. "I just about left."

"Yeah, right." Angel snorted. She'd grown up on the tough streets of East St. Louis, and if he thought these intimidation tactics would keep her in line, he'd best think again.

Crow shot her a sideways glance. "What kept you?"

"A teacher wanted to talk to me."

His gaze sharpened and his eyes glittered like hot coals. "Which one?"

"Jake Weston." Angel popped another piece of gum into her mouth and licked the sticky sweetness from her fingers. "Man, that guy is hot."

Crow's eyes narrowed. "If I didn't know better, I'd think you had a thing for him."

"Me?" Angel laughed. "I'm supposed to be in *high school,* remember? Besides, you know my heart belongs to you." As if to illustrate, she slipped her arm through his and gazed adoringly into his dark-as-midnight eyes.

A look of such disgust crossed his face that Angel couldn't resist a giggle. The sound was so light and carefree, so teen-like, she had to do it again.

Before the second giggle was half out, Crow grabbed her and with one fluid movement deposited her firmly on his lap. Before she could react to the strange turn of events, he lowered his lips and kissed her neck.

Instinctively she pulled back, but his arms tightened around her like steel bands. She struggled, panic welling up from deep inside despite her efforts to squelch it.

"Stop it!" she said with as much force as she could muster and still keep her voice low.

He ignored her and lowered his head, his mouth nuzzling her neck.

"What do you think you're *doing?*"

Had the man flipped out? She increased her efforts and seriously contemplated screaming if his lips dipped any lower.

As if he could read her mind, Crow momentarily lifted his mouth from her skin, an unmistakable warning in his eyes. "Loverboy is on his way."

"Wha—?" Her mouth opened, and Crow's lips closed it.

"Angel?" Jake Weston's voice radiated concern.

She jerked back. This time Crow let her go. Angel tumbled off his lap and onto the bench, her breath coming in short puffs.

"Mr. Weston." Angel resisted the urge to straighten her shirt, and leisurely sat up, meeting his disapproving gaze with a defiant one of her own. "What are you doing here?"

"Do you have a minute?"

Not only didn't he answer her question, but his request sounded suspiciously like a command.

Angel shot a sideways glance at Crow to see if he'd noticed that Jake Weston sounded more like a jealous boyfriend than a concerned teacher. For a second, she swore she saw a hint of amusement in Crow's eyes, but the irritated scowl on his face told her she must have been mistaken.

"I need to talk to you," Jake repeated. "Alone."

Angel hid a smile. If looks could kill, Salvador Tucci would be laid out cold as stone on the bench next to her.

"Crow, babe." Angel ran her hand lightly up his heavily muscled forearm. "I'll catch you later. Okay?"

Crow rose from the bench and pulled Angel up with one hand. He ignored the teacher. There was no kindness in the gaze he fixed on Angel and no hint of an idealistic cop in his steely eyes. "You just make sure you get me what I want."

Without another word to either of them, he turned on his heel and disappeared into the wooded area to the north.

"What he wants?"

"You don't want to know." Four years of working the streets had given Crow a gritty edge, sometimes making the role he played all too believable. Angel's gaze shifted to the now empty playground area. "C'mon, let's swing."

"I don—"

"It's a kick." She grabbed his hand, ignoring the jolt of electricity that surged at the touch. "You've got to try it."

He pulled his hand from her grasp, but followed her to the sandy enclosed area and took a rubber U-shaped swing next to hers.

Instead of pushing off, he twisted in his seat, his gaze thoughtful. "I can't figure you out."

"What you see is what you get." She'd expected him to smile at her response, but he just continued to stare at the mass of chains looped about her neck. Her hand self-consciously rose to cover the silver cross.

"I don't think so." He shook his head. "I think there's a lot more to you than meets the eye."

A shiver traveled down her spine. There was no way he could know. "I'll tell you my secrets," she said. "If you tell me yours…Jake."

"Mr. Weston," he said automatically.

"I like Jake better." She flashed him her most engaging smile.

"Mr. Weston," he said firmly.

Angel scuffed the toe of her shoe into the sand and shook her head. "You're no older than Crow, and he'd split a gut if I called him 'Mister.'"

"That's probably because I'm your teacher and he's your...?"

"Lover?" she offered.

A muscle in his jaw jumped. "Is he?"

"You better believe it," she said.

A startled look crossed his face.

She couldn't help but smile. Jake Weston might turn out to be a drug dealer, but at least the guy cared what she did.

"I still don't understand what you're doing here," she said.

"I live there." He pointed to a distant cluster of apartment buildings. "I was taking a shortcut through the park when I saw you. You looked like you might be in trouble."

Her heart warmed despite herself. In her old neighborhood, no one would have cared, much less stopped to help.

"Thanks," she said softly.

"You're welcome." He glanced around the near-deserted park. "Do you need a lift home?"

"Unless you've got a car hidden in your pocket, I'll pass. I don't think your back could handle me."

He smiled. "We can walk over to my place and pick up my Jeep."

Angel hesitated. "Thanks for the offer, but I'm cool with walking. I might even try to catch Crow."

Jake didn't hide his disapproval. "Angel, you deserve a good life. You're a smart girl. You could make something of yourself."

"If I got rid of Crow," she said with a narrowed glance. "Is that what you're saying?"

"I don't know him, Angel." An uncomfortable look crossed the teacher's face. "But I'm not so sure I like what I see. He's obviously too old for you."

She paused and took a deep breath. Telling a Morelli that they shouldn't do something was tantamount to raising a red flag in front of a bull. But, she rationally reminded herself, the man thought she was a teen and he was only expressing a valid concern. The mature response would be to say nothing.

Still, she *was* supposed to be eighteen, and being young did have some advantages. A girl could be brash and bold and blame it all on immaturity.

"Well," she said airily. "I guess that makes us even."

"Even?"

"You don't think Crow's good for me," she said. "And I don't think that English teacher is good for you."

Jake stood speechless for a moment, before sputtering something about how he and Ms. Delahay were just friends.

Yeah, right. Angel wasn't born yesterday. The beautiful Amanda Delahay looked at Jake like he was a piece of fresh meat and she hadn't eaten in weeks.

Jake continued to stammer. Angel's grin widened. Immensely satisfied by the success of her typical teen response, she stood, waved a cheerful goodbye and, before he could protest, headed off into the woods to look for Crow.

"Tell me you're not serious." Amanda Delahay straightened in her living room chair, a horrified expression on her face.

Jake picked up the glass tumbler from the end table and stared at the tea. He'd thought long and hard before broaching the subject. Now, he wished he'd kept his mouth shut. "I said she needs a mentor. A Big Brother or Big Sister type. I never said it had to be me."

Amanda exhaled a breath that sounded suspiciously like a sigh of relief. "For a moment you had me worried."

"Actually, a woman would be ideal," Jake said thoughtfully, an idea taking shape in his head. "Someone who could be a positive role model."

"I agree," Amanda said matter-of-factly, dusting a piece of lint from her navy slacks. "But good luck finding someone."

Jake leaned forward and grabbed her hand. "It wouldn't be that much work. You cou—"

"Not another word." The blonde jerked her hand from his. "You know how busy I am."

Her jaw set in that stubborn tilt he'd seen before. Jake stifled a groan. He'd moved too fast in his eagerness to sell her on the idea. "You are busy."

"Yes, I am." The tightness around Amanda's mouth eased. "I haven't even made it to the gym once this week."

"You look great." Although the compliment was intended to soothe her ruffled feathers, it was still the truth. With her shoulder-length blond hair, big blue eyes and killer figure, Amanda was one of the most beautiful women he'd ever dated. "You don't need to work out."

Amanda's eyes narrowed suspiciously. "If you think you're going to sweet-talk me into agreeing to take on that—that girl...think again."

"Mandy—"

"Not interested." Amanda held up one hand. "No how. No way."

"C'mon, give it a chance. You'd be a great Big Sister."

"I have a sister, thank you. And Kimberly doesn't wear shirts that are skin-tight and talk sleazy."

"Kimberly's grown up under completely different circumstances," Jake pointed out gently. "This girl hasn't had the same advantages. She deserves a chance."

"Oh, pul-eeze." Amanda rolled her eyes. "I'm sick to death of hearing how someone *deserves* something. Kim and I worked our way through school. No one helped us. No one gave us anything. What this girl needs is to get rid of those trashy clothes, do something with that awful hair and spend a little more time on her studies."

Jake stared. Did she really believe it was that simple? "Amanda, she's a kid living in a foster home, not the girl next door. She needs someone to show her the way. Even in the Bible it—"

"Hold it right there." Amanda's eyes flashed. "I thought your brother's death cured you of that God stuff. Now you're bringing it up again? What's going on?"

Jake took a long sip of his iced tea. From the

start, his faith had been a wall between Amanda and him. When he'd sworn off God after Jim's death, their relationship had deepened. But lately he'd found himself thumbing through the Scriptures, searching for the answers still troubling his soul. "What's going on is…I've started reading my Bible again."

"Oh, Jake." Disappointment rang in her voice. "How can you still believe there's a God after what happened to Jim? He *bled* to death. Where was this God of yours while those little jerks ransacked his apartment and then left him to die?"

"Stop it." He fought the horrible memory. Jim lying in a pool of red. Jim trying to joke while they waited for the ambulance. Jim…dying in his arms. Jake's chest tightened until he could barely breathe.

"I'm just pointing out what you seem so willing to forget." Amanda's voice was soft and not unkind. "If there is a God, why would He let something like that happen?"

"I have no idea." Jake leaned his head back and closed his eyes, a jumble of confusing thoughts and feelings stirring his own doubts. There had been many nights he, too, wondered how a loving God could have allowed his kind and gentle brother to die such a horrible death.

"Think about it, Jake. Those creeps that killed

Jim are living like kings in that new high-class dormitory we call a juvenile facility, watching television and playing pool.'' Amanda snorted in disgust. ''In two years they'll be back on the streets.''

''Three years,'' he said automatically, although he was nowhere near as cool as his tone indicated.

In fact, Jake could barely control his irritation. For months he'd successfully blocked Jim's killers from his memory and he didn't appreciate her bringing it all rushing back. Deep down, he had this crazy notion that if he thought about the two, he might have to forgive them. And that was something he absolutely couldn't do.

''Okay, three years. And Jim is dead forever.'' Amanda swiped her eyes with the back of her hand, and Jake's anger softened. Sometimes he forgot how fond she'd been of his older brother.

''Amanda.'' He reached for her hand, suddenly needing to be close, but she shook her head and wrapped her arms around her body as if the apartment had turned cold.

''I told him an inner-city school was nowhere to be. I told him living in that rat-infested neighborhood was crazy.''

''And he told us he was happy doing the Lord's work.'' Jake's hand dropped to his side. He remembered the Fourth of July picnic vividly.

'' 'Furthering God's kingdom on earth' were his

exact words." Amanda shook her head, bitterness spilling over into her voice. "Look where it got him."

Jake stood abruptly and blinked the moisture from his eyes. "It's getting late."

She looked surprised. "It's barely ten."

"I've got to go." He'd never cried for his brother. Not once. And he certainly wasn't going to cry now.

Amanda grabbed his hand and pulled herself up and into his arms. The light floral scent of her perfume filled his nostrils.

Usually she was impossible to resist.

Jake swiveled and stepped back, breaking the contact. He took a deep breath, fighting for the control that had been his constant companion for the past year. "Like I said, it's getting late."

Her smile never wavered. "Call me tomorrow?"

"If I get a chance." For once he was grateful they usually waited until the last minute to finalize any plans. It made things easier. "I'm going to be pretty busy."

For a long moment she looked at him, then shrugged her shoulders in a nonchalant manner. No one observing them would guess this was the first Saturday night in over a year that they wouldn't spend together.

Amanda accompanied him to the front door, but when he didn't pull her to him for their usual kiss, her fingers curved around his forearm to stop his exit.

"Jake." Regret shone in her eyes, and because he knew her so well, the slight tremble of her lips told him that tonight had been tough on her, too. "I'm sorry if I upset you. I certainly di—"

"Shh." His fingers on her mouth ended her apology. "You've always been honest. I can't fault you for that."

He leaned down and brushed her lips with his. As angry as he was with her, he knew she hadn't meant to open old wounds. She was great. A wonderful woman. Why wasn't it enough anymore?

"Sleep well."

"You, too," she said softly.

He pulled the door shut behind him and leaned against it, utterly drained. He was more burned out than he realized—questioning God, being tempted by a dark-haired Angel, and now fighting with Amanda. Craziness. That's what it was.

Sleep well?

It would be a miracle if he slept at all.

Chapter Three

Who would have thought it would be so hard to scare up a couple of old people?

The clock on the wall chimed six, and Angel grimaced. Jake Weston would be here any minute, and she stood no closer to having some Ben-Gay-laden foster parents to show him than she had been last night when she'd called everyone she could think of and had come up empty.

Still, she wasn't worried. She'd survived for years with her quick thinking, and this was just the sort of challenge she relished.

The doorbell rang, and Angel fluffed her hair with her fingers. She opened the heavily scarred wooden door and punctuated the inward swing with a snap of her gum.

"Jake, my man. C'mon in." She kicked the bottom of the wooden screen door that had a stubborn tendency to stick, and ushered the teacher inside.

His curious gaze slid around the small living room, and she lifted her chin. The department had arranged to rent the place—furniture and all—for next to nothing from a landlord who asked no questions. She'd done her best to make the temporary quarters livable.

The clutter had been vanquished to a back storage shed, and this morning she'd mopped the floors and taken the top layer of dust off the mismatched furniture. The plaster walls were still cracked and peeling, and she couldn't do much about the huge stain on the ceiling from the recent rain—but at least it was clean.

She waved Jake over to the sectional underneath a glow-in-the-dark velvet picture of two praying hands that had come with the furniture.

He sank deep into the soft cushions and glanced toward the hallway. "Are your foster parents…?"

"Gone," she said. "Bowling or something. I told them you were coming but…" She shrugged and let him draw his own conclusions.

His gaze lifted and his expression grew thoughtful. "You lied to me."

"I never said they'd be here."

"I'm not talking about your foster parents." A

glint of humor flashed in the green depths of his eyes. "I'm talking about the Ben-Gay. You said the place reeked of the stuff. It doesn't smell in here at all."

She flashed a saucy smile and lied without skipping a beat. "You can thank me for that. It took a whole can of air freshener, but it worked."

He sniffed. "Pine forest?"

"A dollar forty-nine at Wal-Mart."

He returned her smile, then opened the leather portfolio he'd brought and took out a typewritten form. "We might as well get going on this."

Angel sank down on the sofa next to him and reached for the page. "Let me see."

Her movement brought his face so close that she could feel his breath on her cheek. If the room smelled like a forest, he smelled like spearmint gum and shaving cream. All she needed to do was to turn her head to the side...

He must have read her mind. He stiffened and shifted, effectively moving his lips beyond her reach. "I think it'd be best if you sat over there."

Angel plopped back and crossed her arms over her chest. She glanced at the wooden chair with the rock-hard seat and partially broken arm. "I don't like that one."

"Angel." He glanced pointedly at the chair.

"Okay, be that way." Angel flounced from the

couch and into the chair. It groaned in protest. "See, what'd I tell ya? It hates me as much as I hate it."

He smiled and made a few notes.

She leaned forward and tried to see what he'd written.

He snapped the folder shut.

"What'd you write?" she asked. "Did you say I looked pretty in my new red dress?"

He looked at the clingy crimson fabric, and his eyes darkened. Immediately his gaze shifted to the picture of the praying hands. He cleared his throat.

"It's new," she said, piqued. Had she lost her touch?

"I believe you've already said that."

"I just wanted to make sure you knew." She gazed up at him and fluttered her eyelashes, feeling awkward and just a little bit stupid.

He studied her for a moment. "Do you have something in your eye?"

"No, I do not have som—" She noticed the smile tugging at his lips and shut her mouth.

The bare bulb overhead reflected the emerald of his eyes, and a shiver of excitement coursed through her body.

"Tonight is a special occasion," she said. "A very special one."

"Really?" Jake flipped open the folder.

Angel smiled, and her heart hammered foolishly in her chest. Flirting was even more fun than she'd remembered. She lowered her voice to a husky whisper. "It's special because you're here. I wore the dress for you."

Startled, his eyes widened. A flush started at the base of his neck and spread upward. He fumbled for his pen. "It's very nice."

Satisfied, Angel's smile widened and she snapped her gum. "Thanks."

"O-kay." Jake expelled a pent-up breath. "Let's get going here."

Angel kept her gaze focused on his face and listened to him stumble his way through an overview of Woodland Hills High School's at-risk program. She refrained from making any suggestions, even though there were a dozen ways that the program could be improved at very little additional cost.

"You don't have *any* questions?"

Her head jerked up, and she realized he'd quit speaking. A smile hovered on the edge of his lips as if he knew her mind had wandered.

She thought quickly and latched onto one of the last things he'd mentioned. "About this mentor thing—"

"It means—"

"I know what it means." Impatiently she waved

him silent. "What I want to know is—who do I get stuck with?"

He shifted uncomfortably. "Actually, that hasn't been determined."

With an irritation that wasn't all forced, Angel crossed her legs, exposing a long stretch of skin. "Don't tell me nobody wants me."

His look answered her question.

In spite of herself, in spite of knowing this was all pretend, her heart twisted. An unexplained wave of sadness washed over her. It must have shown on her face, because Jake leaned forward, his arms resting on his thighs, compassion lighting his eyes. "Angel, you've got a lot of potential. We'll find someone."

"Yeah, right."

"We will," he said firmly.

She gazed into his handsome caring face, and the stirrings of a brilliant idea blossomed. "Why don't you do it?"

It was the perfect solution. If he was her mentor, she could stay close to him without arousing suspicion.

"I don't think that would be a good idea."

Angel paused and raised a brow. "Why not?"

"I just don't think it would."

"Because you like me too much?"

"I like all my students," he said slowly and deliberately. "I just think you might do better with a woman."

"I've always gotten along better with men than women."

"Angel." She had to hide a smile at the almost parental admonishment.

"Jaaake," Angel mimicked, and smiled when his lips finally curved with amusement.

"You're not making this easy." He raked his fingers through his hair. "I really don't have time. The baseball team keeps me busy."

Angel's ears perked up. Crow had gotten a tip that some of the students dealing drugs were part of the team. Although these kids would be small fish, they might point her to the leader.

This was all too perfect. Her heart skipped a beat.

"I'd love to help out." Angel tossed her head and shot him an impish smile. "All the hot guys play baseball."

"I thought you already had a boyfriend," Jake said. Angel stared blankly.

"Crow?" he prompted.

"Oh, him." Angel waved a hand. "He's my main man, but there's nothing to say a girl can't look."

"It *might* be best if you had a boyfriend your

own age," Jake said in an offhand manner that she guessed was anything but offhand.

"I like my men more mature," she said coyly.

He winced. "Angel, listen to me—"

She could smell a lecture coming a mile away. "I'm bored." She stood and the chair creaked. "Let's grab a burger. We'll talk later. I'm starving." As if on cue, her stomach growled.

Jake shifted. He glanced down at his open notepad. "We barely got started."

"Bring the stuff along." She hopped up and reached for his hand. "Big Al's Burger Palace is just down the block. We can talk while we walk."

He stayed seated. "I don't think it'd be a good idea for us to be seen out together on a Saturday night. People might get the wrong idea."

Angel stared at him thoughtfully. He seemed like such a good guy. She sighed heavily. "All right. PB&J it is. You can have one, too."

"Thanks, but I already ate."

He followed her into the kitchen, and she grabbed bread and peanut butter from the cupboard, dumping them onto the counter with a clatter. Without thinking, she swung open the refrigerator door in search of the jelly.

Jake's gaze narrowed at the sight of the empty shelves, and Angel bit her lip. Why hadn't she thought to fill it? The last thing she needed was for him to make a referral to Social Services.

"Grocery day is tomorrow," she said, abruptly closing the door.

Jake looked skeptical, but what else could she say? She only prayed she'd convinced him.

Angel quickly threw together a sandwich and grabbed a couple of warm cans of soda from the open carton on top of the counter. She tossed one across the table with an underhand lob. Jake caught it easily. She gave him a quick thumbs-up and took the chair across the table.

While she ate, they talked. Surprisingly, the conversation flowed easily, and Angel discovered that Jake had a sense of humor in sync with her own.

Only when she deliberately inserted a joke about getting high did she strike out. His smile faded and his gaze turned sharp and assessing.

"Drugs are a dead end," he said flatly.

His expression gave nothing away, and once again she wished she could read his mind. Did he spout the platitude because it was expected or did he really mean it?

"Ya think?"

His gaze swept her face. "What do *you* think, Angel?"

"Me?" She forced a laugh. "Haven't you heard? I'm high on life."

He stared thoughtfully and opened his mouth before closing it. A chill ran down her spine. Had he been about to lecture her? Or could it be that Crow was right?

Was Jake Weston their man?

And if he was, what was she going to do about it?

The clock struck ten. Angel dialed Crow's number from memory. He answered on the first ring.

"It's Angel. He just left."

"Stayed long enough." Crow spoke gruffly, bringing a smile to her lips. Her partner had taken an instant dislike to Jake. "Find out anything?"

She hesitated.

"Don't jerk me around, Angel," he said in that rough guttural voice she'd come to know so well. "Give it to me straight."

"I brought up getting high." She twisted the bed sheet between her fingers. It had been a calculated maneuver, not an off-the-wall comment. But she wasn't sure Crow would see it that way.

"You *what?*"

She held the receiver away from her ear for a second before pressing it back into place. "I was *subtle.*"

"I bet." His disbelieving laugh carried across the phone lines. "So what do you think?"

"I'm not sure," she said, trying to be completely honest. "I couldn't get a good feel. My gut says no."

"Your gut has been wrong before," he said, his tone uncharacteristically gentle.

Even so, his words stung. "I found out he's a Christian." When she'd mentioned her friend Emily attended Woodland Hills Community Church, she'd been surprised to learn Jake was also a member.

"I don't care if he's God Almighty." Crow snorted. "You need to quit talkin' religion and find out who can get you the meth. Cozy up to him. Whatever it takes. We're running out of time."

Angel hung up the phone and leaned her head against the worn velvet of the couch. Getting close to Jake would be easy. There was a bond, an inexplicable attraction between them that she'd never expected.

No, getting close would be the least of her current problems. And more than likely, just the beginning of a whole set of new ones.

Chapter Four

Angel's glance slid from the blue solution to the clock on the wall. Science had never been one of her strengths.

"You're new here, huh?"

Her attention jerked to Emily Weyer, her lab partner, taking in the girl's tentative smile and anxious expression. Up to now they'd worked alone on the experiments, but today Mr. Monk—whom everyone not-so-affectionately called Mr. Monkey—had made them pair off. By default, she and this girl had ended up together.

"Yeah, how 'bout you?" Angel cast a wary eye at the beaker. She'd never realized until last week how fast a fire could start. Perhaps that's why Mr. Monkey had insisted they take partners.

The girl nodded, and Angel quickly assessed her. Brown shoulder-length hair, blue eyes and regular features; she would blend into any crowd without a problem.

It was an advantage Angel wished she could claim. Unfortunately her own hair was too dark, her eyes too large and her mouth too full to go unnoticed. She grimaced.

Emily quickly took a step back. "I'm sorry. We don't have to talk."

If the girl didn't look so intimidated, Angel would have had to laugh. Instead she smiled. "Of course we do. We're women, aren't we? Besides, it gets boring just watching this stuff."

Angel gestured expansively to the Bunsen burner, her sleeve coming precariously close to the blue flame. She jerked her arm back just in time.

"Changing schools your senior year is kind of hard." Emily glanced around the room. "Most kids already have their friends. And they don't seem too interested in making any new ones."

"Bummer," Angel said. She'd had the same experience. It had made her job doubly hard. She glanced at the beaker and wondered if Emily knew what they were supposed to do next.

"It doesn't bother you." Amazement and something akin to admiration rang in the girl's hushed whisper. "Not at all."

Angel hesitated. It hadn't been that long ago that being on the outside had mattered a lot. And not only had she felt all alone at school, but she'd felt that way at home, too. Her aunt and uncle hadn't wanted her. The foster parents hadn't wanted her. She shoved the painful memories aside and reminded herself that that time in her life hadn't been all bad.

"Not at all," Angel echoed, and turned her gaze from the now-boiling liquid for a fraction of a second.

The beaker shattered and hot liquid flooded the counter. Emily screamed. Angel jumped back as shards of glass flew through the air. Mr. Monkey roared. Chaos erupted.

Fifteen minutes later they finally finished the cleanup. After a stern lecture from Mr. Monkey, who resembled an angry gorilla when he screamed something about the importance of listening to instructions, the two girls were finally released to the now-empty hall.

"He was really mad," Emily said.

Angel shrugged. "I could have sworn he said it was supposed to boil."

"Do you think he'll have it out for us now?"

"Who knows?" Angel tossed her backpack strap over one shoulder. "Do monkeys hold grudges?"

Her words brought a smile to the girl's face.

"You wouldn't want to—" Emily swallowed hard "—have lunch with me? We could eat in the commons?"

Woodland Hills High School had been built in a square with an open inner courtyard. Although Angel hadn't spent much time sitting under the big leafy trees, she knew it was considered *the* place to gather for students and staff.

Angel glanced at her watch. She'd hoped to make a few quick calls before her next class. "I don't..."

The girl's expression fell and the hope in her eyes died a quick death.

"Even as you do this unto the least of my brethren..."

Angel rested a hand on Emily's shoulder. "On second thought, why not?"

They walked companionably down the quiet halls and out into the bright sunshine. A shaded area under a huge sycamore beckoned, and Angel claimed the spot against the tree. Emily sat across from her and pulled a brown sack from her satchel, splitting half of its contents with Angel.

The bologna sandwich was dry, the apple soft, and the brownie clung to Angel's fingers like glue. Still, it was food—and she hadn't eaten since the previous night.

"You're a senior, right?" Angel licked her fingers and rested her back against the rough bark. She cast the girl an interested look, and that's all it took.

Once Emily started talking, it was like the floodwaters had been released. She wouldn't shut up. In a matter of minutes Angel discovered that for being new and living on the fringes, Emily had already gathered a wealth of information about her fellow classmates. Information Angel found extremely interesting.

"Hey, Em, you're lookin' good." A tall slender boy with short brown hair tipped with gold slowed, then continued walking when he caught sight of Angel. Angel got the distinct feeling he would have stopped if Emily had been alone.

"Mike." Emily smiled and dipped her head as if to hide the blush stealing its way up her cheeks.

"Who's that?" Angel asked, the boy's face naggingly familiar. "He's way cute."

"You don't know Mike Blaine?" Shock blanketed the girl's face. "Everybody knows Mike."

"I don't." Angel licked the rest of the brownie's caramel topping off her fingers, pleased she could sound so calm.

The instant Emily had said his name, it had all come rushing back. Mike Blaine had been named by informants as a dealer.

"He's the shortstop on the baseball team," Emily said proudly.

Angel forced a smile, wondering if she should give more credence to the rumors about a connection between the baseball team and the drug ring. "Isn't Jake Weston the coach?"

Emily shrugged. "I guess."

Obviously the teacher hadn't made quite the impression the hunky shortstop had. "Mike's hot."

"Yeah," Emily said. "And he's pretty nice, too."

"Do you guys have something going?"

A look Angel couldn't quite identify crossed Emily's face. "I think he'd like to, but—"

A burst of laughter carried across the grassy expanse, and Emily and Angel turned in unison. Mike stood in front of the school doors surrounded by five or six friends. Angel mentally catalogued the companions before turning her attention back to Emily.

"You were saying?"

Emily's blush deepened. "It's sort of personal."

Angel raised a brow.

"He and I don't agree on…well, on a lot of things."

"Let me guess." Angel placed a finger to her lips and pretended to think, even though she had no doubt her first instinct would nail it. "Mike wants sex and you don't."

Emily's eyes widened. "How did you know?"

Angel lifted one shoulder in a slight shrug. "What guy doesn't want sex?"

"You probably think I'm being stupid." Emily stared down at her pastel-pink-tipped nails. "Truth is, I don't plan to do that with anyone until I'm married."

"Really?" Angel tilted her head and gazed speculatively at Emily.

"You agree with him." Disappointed resignation rang in Emily's voice.

"Actually—" Angel shot an apple core in a high arch right into a nearby trash can "—I agree with you."

"You do?"

"Yep." Angel nodded. "Matter of fact, I'm doing the same thing."

"Uh-huh." Emily started to laugh, but stopped when Angel didn't smile. "You're serious?"

"Sure I am." Angel stared intently at Emily and wished she could share more with the girl—but she couldn't risk blowing her cover.

Emily shook her head. "I never would have guessed."

Angel gave a careless wave. "So, is that all? The guy wants sex and you don't?"

Emily shifted uncomfortably and refused to meet Angel's questioning gaze. "Pretty much."

"No, it's not. I can tell," Angel said, her interest piqued. "We're friends. You can tell me."

"He'd be mad if he knew I said anything."

Angel leaned forward and made a show of zipping her lips. "You can trust me."

Emily glanced around as if to make sure no one could overhear. Apparently reassured, she lowered her voice almost to a whisper. "Mike and I went out a couple of times. He wanted more from me, but he took me saying no, okay. I mean he was disappointed but..."

"But...?"

"It was the other we couldn't agree on."

"Other?" Angel prompted.

"Drugs." Emily spoke so low that the word could barely be heard.

Excitement shot through Angel like a lightning bolt.

"I know crank—" Emily stumbled over the word "—is popular with some, but..."

"It's not for you."

Emily's blue eyes were intense. "No."

"Does he sell the stuff?" Angel said in an offhand manner. She hoped she wasn't too transparent.

"Why?" Emily said bluntly. "You want to buy some? That's it, isn't it?"

"Maybe," Angel said, wishing she could somehow erase the disappointment reflected in Emily's clear-eyed gaze.

"Yeah, he deals, too," Emily said reluctantly.

"Could you fix me up?" Angel could barely contain herself. Crow would be pumped.

"How would I do that without him knowing I told you?"

"Just introduce me," Angel said. "I'll take it from there."

"You must like it, too," Emily said, sounding thoughtful. "Mike said it'd help me keep my weight down. Said I'd like it, if I just gave it a chance."

Concern twisted Angel's gut. "I'm getting it for a friend."

"You are?"

"Yeah, my friend's all about crystal. Me, I like to keep my body pure. You know, God's temple and all that."

Emily stared as if she wasn't sure if Angel was jerking her around or being serious. "I could introduce you tonight at the party for the baseball team," Emily said. "There'll be pizza and pop there. They won some tournament, and the whole school's invited."

"Perfect." Angel picked up her bag and slung it over her shoulder. "What time shall I pick you up?"

"Angel. I didn't expect to see you." Jake Weston's voice sounded behind her, and Angel jumped.

She turned slowly and willed her heart to slow. "Jake, my man."

"Mr. Weston," Jake said. "Or Coach."

As if to illustrate, a gangly boy who couldn't have been more than a freshman yelled across the crowd, "Coach. We need more plates."

Jake heaved a sigh and waved a hand in acknowledgment. "I better go get them."

Despite his words, he made no move to leave.

"Where to?" she said, her gaze riveted to his.

"My Jeep." He jerked his head toward the park's gravel lot. "Over there."

The lights from the halogens overhead cast streaks of gold through his hair. She resisted the urge to brush a stray strand back from his forehead. "I'll go with you." Angel wrapped her arm around his.

Without saying a word, he firmly removed it. She shrugged and gave him a saucy smile.

He headed toward the parking lot, and she had to almost run to get in front of him. Once there, she slowed her pace, keeping only a few feet between them. Angel swung her hips from side to side, knowing his eyes had to be fixed firmly on her. She smiled, feeling strangely lighthearted and carefree.

Maybe it was this change-of-image thing. She was sick to death of the type of clothing she'd worn the last three weeks—sloppy jeans that threatened to drop to the ground or spandex clinging so tight she could barely breathe. The dress she had on tonight more closely mirrored the type of attire she preferred to wear.

She and Emily had picked up the simple cotton sundress at the mall after school. The white eyelet enhanced her olive skin and made her hair look jet black. The dress wasn't tight or loose, but just right, and when her new friend had gushed on and on about how cute she looked in it, what could she do but buy it?

If Emily was right and Mike was a dealer, these changes were necessary. She certainly would never fit in with his crowd in what she'd been wearing. An added bonus was that she had a hunch Jake Weston might be impressed with her new look, though he'd never admit it.

"Do you like my dress?"

"Didn't you ask me that the last time I saw you?"

"Maybe," she said. "But this is a different one. The other was red."

He glanced at the short white sundress, his gaze lingering on the spaghetti straps. "It's nice."

"I wore it just for you."

"I think I've heard that before."

"I'm aiming for a different look," she said, and twirled in the darkness, her skirt flaring out.

"What does Crow think about these changes?"

"I don't know. I haven't asked him." Angel leaned back against his Jeep. "Right now, I don't care."

He raised an eyebrow but remained silent.

"I just bought some new lip gloss. It's watermelon flavored," she said playfully.

Jake's eyes darkened, and for a second the world ceased to exist. He closed the distance between them until he stood so near that she could feel his breath on her face. A tightness gripped her belly. She raised a hand and touched his arm.

Laughter erupted across the lot, and Jake froze. He blinked as if just waking up. He took a step back. And then another.

Her hand fell to her side.

"Angel, this has to stop."

"What?"

"Don't play the innocent," he said. "You can't keep coming on to me."

She ran a finger along his jaw. "Why? 'Fraid you'll give in?"

His muscle twitched in his cheek. "You're eighteen years old."

"I'm mature for my age."

"You're still a student and I'm a teacher."

"You get hung up on the strangest things," she said with a laugh. "All right, have it your way. For now."

She flashed him an impudent grin and headed back to the party, feeling his eyes follow her the entire way.

Amanda Delahay watched Jake from a distance. A breeze ruffled his hair, and he brushed it back without taking his eyes off a young man Amanda recognized as one of his baseball players.

Jake was so intense, so committed to his players. It was that intensity that had drawn her to him when she first met him. She'd transferred to Woodland Hills High a little over a year ago, and Jake, with his blond good looks and engaging personality, had caught her eye immediately.

They'd started dating soon after they met. And through him she'd met Jim. If Jake was handsome, his older brother Jim was gorgeous. If Jake was pleasant, Jim was dynamic. And if Jake had caught her eye, Jim had captured her heart.

Not that Jim had ever let her close, she thought morosely. She was Jake's girl, Jim had told her when she'd dared to voice her feelings shortly before he'd been killed. And even if she weren't, he'd gently told her, he could never enter into a relationship with someone who didn't share his religious faith.

It would have been a problem with Jake, too, if Jim hadn't died. But for almost a year Jake had turned his back on his faith. Now that had changed, and Amanda couldn't be more confused. How such an educated man couldn't see that religion was nothing more than organized superstition was beyond her.

Still, she liked Jake. She noticed him flashing a smile at that dark-haired minx. Her heart turned over. Before that girl showed up and ruined everything, Jake had looked at her that way.

And he would again.

Amanda straightened. She certainly wasn't going to let a year-long relationship end without a fight and she wasn't going to see him put his job on the line for some high school student. The fact that the faith issue still stood between them was put in her favorite "to be dealt with later" file.

She adjusted her skirt, fluffed her hair with her fingers and headed across the picnic area toward Jake.

"Hi, handsome." Amanda sent him her most engaging smile, relieved at finding him alone. "Can I join you?"

A guarded look shuttered his gaze. "Amanda, I don't think—"

"Thanks." She sat on the bench across from him and didn't give him a chance to protest. "How've you been?"

"Hey, Coach, I'm going to go pick up some more pizzas." The boy that had been talking to Jake earlier interrupted.

"Drive carefully."

Amanda waited until the boy was out of earshot before she spoke. "I'm not sure why you haven't called but we still have to work together. Even if we don't date, I still want to be your friend. Is that too much to ask?"

He hesitated, and she held her breath. When he smiled, she knew she'd cracked open the door.

"I never wanted us to not be friends," he said.

"Well, friend." She tilted her head and reached across the table for his plate. "How about sharing a slice of that pizza?"

"Coach must not like pizza," Angel said to Emily and Mike in what she hoped was an offhand manner. For the past hour she'd watched Jake out of the corner of her eye. He'd talked to a lot of people, but had merely pushed his food around his plate.

"He used to like it." The handsome jock cast a sideways glance at his coach. "But he's different this year."

"How's that?" Angel pried a piece of pepperoni from the roof of her mouth with her tongue.

"Doesn't like pizza."

Angel hid her irritation and reminded herself he was just eighteen. "How else?"

Mike shrugged and thought for a moment. "Things get to him more. Yesterday a couple of guys were horsing around in the bullpen. Coach caught 'em, and they had to run laps. Last year he wouldn't have cared. Still, he's a good enough guy." Mike dropped the rest of his slice to the paper plate in front of him and shoved the plate aside. "I've had enough."

The look he shot Emily said that although he may have lost his appetite for food, he was still…hungry.

Mike pushed back his chair and stood, then reached down and pulled Emily up with one hand. "Em and I are going to take a walk."

Angel shot the girl an assessing look, somewhat mollified when she smiled back.

"We won't be gone long," Emily said.

"Hey, don't tell me. I'm not your mom." Angel

waved them off and reached for her pizza. She'd only had a few bites and her stomach growled in anticipation. The spicy scent of sausage and pepperoni mingled with the aroma of cheese and tomatoes.

She bit into the thick crust and stopped, her gaze settling on a couple tables over.

Jake and Amanda Delahay sat across from each other.

Angel's stomach churned.

The pretty blonde lifted her face and must have said something funny, because they both laughed.

Angel swallowed hard and dropped the pizza to the plate, not able to eat another bite.

As if they could feel her staring, they turned. Angel smiled and gave them a jaunty wave.

Jake waved back. Amanda turned away. Angel shifted her gaze.

This night was going downhill fast. For the most part Mike had ignored her, and she was no closer to Jake Weston than before. In fact, she worried that her boldness might have put him off completely.

She dreaded tonight's conversation with Crow. He'd been counting on her to bring him the goods, and she didn't have squat. But somehow, someway she'd come up with something.

She'd make the contacts she needed.
She'd get her hands on those drugs.
No matter what it took.
She had no other choice.

Chapter Five

"What kind of game are you playing, Jake?" Amanda's gaze narrowed. "Last week you said we could be friends."

"Mandy." He covered her hand with his and wished for a better way to handle this difficult task. "I want to be your friend. But I can't go to that party with you. We're no longer a couple."

"You acted glad to see me!" Her voice rang with accusation. "You put your arm around me."

He'd been wrong to think they could be just friends. "I didn't realize—"

She swiped her eyes with the back of her hand and glared. "It's her, isn't it?"

A sinking feeling gripped his stomach but he

met her gaze head-on. "I don't know what you're talking about."

"Hah!" Amanda's staccato bark barely qualified as a laugh and carried with it not one hint of amusement.

His anger surged. Though he knew exactly what she was getting at, Jake refused to give her wild charges any credence. "C'mon, be reasonable."

"I am reasonable. I'm not the one interested in children."

He pushed back his desk chair with a clatter and stood, his hands clenched into tight fists. "This discussion is over."

"What's the matter?" she taunted, her pretty face twisted. "Hitting too close to home?"

Jake shook his head, not trusting himself to speak. It had been a long time since he'd been so disappointed in a friend. How could she, who knew him so well, even think such a thing?

Granted, they were very different people. He'd often wondered how they'd ended up dating at all. In the beginning, he'd been sure she'd been interested in someone else. But then Jim had died, and she hadn't left his side. He couldn't have asked for someone more supportive. And when her father had died a month later, he'd returned the kindness. He realized now that they'd been two souls in need of someone to heal their pain. The problem was, they'd made the mistake of turning to each other rather than to Christ.

"I'm right, aren't I? You want that child."

His gaze met Amanda's, and he forced himself to look beyond the anger and see instead the hurt and confusion. He sat down and raked his fingers through his hair. Unfortunately, understanding where this was coming from didn't make it any easier to bear.

"Amanda, listen. You know me too well to be making such accusations."

"I *thought* I knew you." She lifted her chin and tossed her head defiantly. "I'm not so sure anymore."

Jake blew a harsh breath. "I want you to leave. When you're ready to be rational you come back, and we'll talk."

She started to protest, but he waved her words aside. "My next class is in fifteen minutes. It will have to be later."

With all the bearing of a queen, Amanda rose. She flipped a strand of hair over her shoulder, then leaned forward, bracing one hand against his desktop. "Just be careful, Jake. Be very careful."

He let her go, relief flooding him when she pulled the door shut behind her. If she had stayed much longer, he might have said something he would regret. Still, what nerve! To suggest he had a personal interest in Angel Morelli was beyond ludicrous.

He had been a teacher long enough to know the boundaries that must never be crossed between teacher and student, despite any misplaced attractions. And he could guarantee to Amanda and to anyone else with such crazy notions that Jake Weston would never venture one step over that line!

With all the righteousness of a man who knows what he stands for, Jake dismissed Amanda and her words from his thoughts. He pulled out his plan book and focused instead on the upcoming lesson.

"Coach?"

Jake's head jerked up. A freshman who'd failed to make the baseball team stood in the doorway, his Adam's apple bobbing in his too-thin neck. "Could you come here for a minute?"

Jake sighed and pushed aside the book, resigned to sticking with his original lesson plan.

He followed the boy out into the hall.

"It's over there. I was on my way to the media center when I saw it." The gangly freshman pointed at a purple backpack propped against a locker. The teen's voice lowered. "Do you think it's a bomb?"

Jake recognized the backpack immediately. Angel was the only student who carried one like it.

"Maybe we should call the police." The boy's

voice cracked and his expression was so anxious, Jake's heart went out to him.

Making the leap from abandoned backpack to bomb seemed a bit overreactive. Still, with all the violence involving young people these days, one couldn't be too careful.

"You did the right thing in coming to me." Jake clapped a hand on the boy's shoulder and smiled reassuringly. "But I think I know who it belongs to. Her locker's right in this area."

They talked companionably for a few minutes before Jake sent the boy back to his homeroom with an excuse why a trip to pick up a book had taken so long.

Jake picked up the backpack and brought it into his classroom, dropping it on his desk with a *thud*. It weighed a ton. If he had to guess, he'd say it carried her entire day's supply of books. Why she hadn't missed it by now was a mystery. Assuming, of course, that this was actually her bag.

His gaze returned to rest speculatively on the purple nylon. It was the spitting image of Angel's, right down to the unique white stripe on the front flap. But the actual brand was a popular one, and this was a big school. It could conceivably belong to someone else.

A thought struck him, and it was so obvious he

almost laughed. Why didn't he just look and make sure it was hers?

He slid open the zipper. As he'd surmised, the bag was jammed full with textbooks. Jake carefully pulled the heavy volumes out and looked in each for a name in the front jacket or a paper with a name stuffed inside. He searched them one by one until they sat stacked on the corner of his desk in a single neat pile. All that remained in the bottom were a few pennies and one nickel.

Jake frowned. No name in the books. No papers. Not one stick of identification. He'd have expected a wallet, or at least a driver's license, to be in the bag.

Resigned to the fact that he wouldn't know for sure until he saw her during last period and could ask her, he picked a book from the pile and shoved it into the opening. His fingers brushed against an inner pocket. He'd had a similar backpack in college and had often used that hidden compartment for storing extra cash. Perhaps this owner kept her—or his—identification inside.

The flap opened easily, and Jake stuck his hand into the small place, reminding himself he wasn't doing anything improper. He needed to confirm the rightful owner so he could return the bag as soon as possible.

In seconds, a Missouri driver's license, a tattered

picture and a twenty-dollar bill lay in the palm of his hand.

Jake couldn't take his eyes off the photograph. A wilder, much younger Angel stared back at him. Dressed in an off-the-shoulder blouse and jeans, she looked to be no more than fifteen. Her hair bushed out in all directions, and thick black eyeliner encircled both eyes. Lipstick darkened her mouth, and rouge applied with a heavy hand colored her cheeks. She looked, Jake thought, like a young streetkid. But it was the innocence behind the smile that tugged on Jake's heartstrings and told him, even at a young age, Angel wasn't as wild as she appeared.

His gaze slid over the boy with his arm looped around Angel's bare shoulder. Jake moved the picture into closer view—and froze.

What was that substitute teacher they'd had last semester doing with Angel?

Jake paused, collecting his thoughts. It couldn't be Tony D'Fusco. The kid in the picture and Angel looked about the same age. Tony had to be a good six years older than her.

Perhaps this little hoodlum with his long hair, arrogant sneer and cigarette dangling from his lips was Tony's younger brother—though it seemed improbable that the clean-cut Tony, who didn't smoke and was a health nut, could have such a brother.

Tired of speculating, Jake turned his attention to the driver's license. Angel was lucky—it looked like her. Unlike his driver's photo, which made him look like a cross between a concentration camp prisoner and a deranged ghost.

Yes, he thought, staring intently at the picture. Angel should keep this one as long as possible. His gaze idly shifted to the date of birth field. He paused, blinked and refocused his gaze. According to this, Angel and he were the same age!

He shook his head. After class, they were going to have a talk. Maybe after he got through chewing her out for having a fake ID, he'd ask her about the picture. Maybe find out if that kid was any relation to Tony.

Jake picked up the picture and studied it more closely. He flipped it over. In childish scrawl written across the back in purple pen, were the words *Me and Tony,* along with the year.

Jake took a deep breath and willed his heart to slow. It didn't make sense. Why was Angel at Woodland Hills High, pretending to be eighteen when she was really twenty-six?

He started to shove the license and picture into the bag's pocket, then stopped and carefully placed them along with the money exactly as he'd found them. He then did the same with the books, until they were all back in place.

Now he had two mysteries on his hands—Angel and Tony D'Fusco.

"There's no one on this staff that would be involved in drug dealing." The words he'd spoken to the police officers when they'd interviewed him came rushing back.

He'd never thought about the substitute staff. Tony had been a regular all last semester, but Jake hadn't seen him since before Christmas.

Jake sat up straight. Tony had quit filling in right around the time the police had placed the first undercover cop. It seemed almost too coincidental.

But if Tony was involved, wouldn't that mean Angel was, too? Of course, she could just as easily be an undercover cop. Although he couldn't imagine the diminutive Angel in a police uniform with a gun strapped to her side. Deep in his heart, he couldn't believe she was a drug dealer, either. He shook his head. What was there about him that made him believe the best of people? He'd always been a soft touch.

Just like my brother.

The thought twisted inside him. Jim had trusted his students and lost his life because of that misplaced trust. Jake wouldn't be so foolish. He'd get to the bottom of this mystery before he made any judgments. And Tony D'Fusco would be the key.

After school today, he'd make a few calls. He hoped he'd be able to talk to Tony and find out his connection to Angel. Then he'd know for sure which side of the law Angel was on.

He couldn't deny that he was relieved Angel wasn't eighteen. Amanda had been right when she'd hinted he had more than a teacherly interest in the girl, er, woman.

Still, despite all that, if she *was* involved in an illegal activity—Angel Morelli was going to be one sorry angel.

He'd see to it.

Angel sucked the last of her chocolate shake through the straw, using the time to gather her thoughts.

"So, what do you think?" Crow leaned over the gray Formica countertop that separated them, clearly impatient.

Part of what made him edgy, Angel knew, was where they'd been seated. Sitting at a table in the middle of the room might not bother most people, but she and Crow, like most cops, didn't like to have their backs exposed. They'd chosen this out-of-the-way place because of its location. How were they to know this ramshackle building with its peeling white paint and weathered sign proclaiming Burger and Fries—CHEAP was a favorite of laborers from a nearby construction site?

Now it was too late to go anywhere else. She was already missing most of her afternoon classes.

"What do I think?" Angel leaned forward and lowered her voice. "Mike's definitely dealing. There might be a few other athletes involved, as well."

Crow's dark eyes gleamed. "Finally we're getting somewhere. What about Weston?"

"Jake?" Angel pushed the plate that still held most of a double cheeseburger to one side. "I'm not sure."

"Right now he's our prime suspect."

"I know that, Crow." Her voice came out sharper than she intended. "I'm not stupid."

The knowing look he gave her sent her blood pressure soaring. She'd spent the past few years proving to her colleagues on the force that she was as good as they were, and she resented Crow acting as if she was letting her emotions get in the way of her doing her job.

Angel took a deep breath and forced a reasonable tone. "I'm moving as fast as I can. But remember, he's a teacher and he thinks I'm a student."

Crow's harsh bark of a laugh took her by surprise. "Get real. He's a guy and he's got it bad for you, student or not."

Although Crow's words should have pleased her, Angel was disturbed. She found Jake Weston attractive, and because *she* knew she wasn't an eighteen-year-old high school student she had no problem trying to establish a relationship with him. But he was a teacher and he thought she was a teen. If he did respond, her respect for him would plummet.

"Okay, I'll step up my efforts. If he's involved, I'll find out."

"You're doing a good job, Angel," Crow said. "I'd never guess, if I didn't know, that this is your first time undercover."

His comment pleased her. Crow wasn't one to offer undeserved praise. "I'm just glad my cousin is no longer subbing at Woodland. He'd blow my cover in seconds."

Crow took a sip of coffee so dark that it gave new meaning to the word *black*. "Where is he now?"

"Italy. He's teaching English at an international school over there."

The waitress came over, and to Angel's surprise, Crow accepted a refill. It wasn't often he sat and talked after they'd concluded their business.

"I don't even know any of my cousins," Crow mused.

Angel understood. With the breakdown of the nuclear family, very few of the teens she'd counseled had much contact with any of their extended family.

"I lived with my aunt and uncle for a while when I was fifteen." Angel shook her head. "You should have seen my cousin and me back then. We made quite a pair. I looked like I ran around the streets, and Tony...well, he looked a lot like you do now." The minute the words left Angel's lips, she wished she could snatch them back.

Crow laughed. "That bad?"

"I have this photo I should show you." She stuck her hand in the pocket of her jeans before she remembered she'd left it, along with her driver's license, tucked safely inside her backpack.

"What's the matter? Change your mind?"

"No, I didn't change my mind." Angel laughed. The picture was bad, but not *that* bad. "I left it in my bag. I'll show you when we get back to the car."

Crow's brow furrowed. "Your bag isn't in my car."

"Sure, it is," Angel said promptly. "I had it with me when you picked me up at the school."

"No." Crow spoke slowly and deliberately. "You didn't."

An icy chill gripped Angel's heart. "Are you sure?"

"Positive." His gaze sharpened. "What did you have in it?"

She forced herself to breathe normally and to think logically. "I stopped by my locker after my last class. I know I had it then. But I can't remember if I took the bag into the bathroom with me."

"I didn't ask *where*," Crow said. "I asked *what*. Is there anything in there you wouldn't want anyone to see?"

Despite her fear, Angel recognized that Crow was showing remarkable restraint. Of course, he didn't yet realize she'd done something that had the potential to blow the whole investigation.

She took a deep breath. "Just a picture of Tony and me. But I doubt anyone would recognize him. And even if they did, it shouldn't matter."

"That's all? Just a picture of you and your cousin?"

She hesitated. "And my driver's license."

Crow's voice was low and taut. "The one showing your real age?"

Angel nodded.

An expletive burst from Crow's lips like a gunshot, and his palm hit the table with a resounding *smack.* "How could you be so stupid? Don't you have a brain?"

Heads turned, and Angel realized they'd unwittingly captured the attention of the entire restaurant. Two burly construction workers slid out of their booth, casting murderous glances at Crow. They took a step forward, and Angel could see they meant to defend her against the enraged bull across the table.

She had to defuse the situation. And fast.

Without a moment's hesitation, Angel pushed herself up just far enough to allow her to lean over the cluttered table and kiss Crow full on the lips. While he was still sputtering, she took full advantage of the moment.

She stroked his cheek with one hand, grateful he didn't bat it away, and raised her voice to a sultry whisper loud enough to be overheard. "Sweetie, don't be such a bear. Why don't we go over to your place, and I promise I'll make it up to you."

Crow was quick. Angel could see by the look in his eyes that he realized the seriousness of the situation.

He laced his fingers through her hair with one hand and brought her face closer for another kiss, before answering in that whiskey voice, "I'm all yours, babe."

Catcalls and whistles accompanied their walk out of the café and across the rocky lot to their car.

Only when she was safely ensconced in the high-performance Ford's front seat did Angel relax. She leaned her head back and cast her partner a sideways glance. "I'm sorry, Crow."

He slid behind the steering wheel. "You did good back there. That was some quick thinking."

"I mean about leaving the backpack. It was inexcusable."

The engine roared to life, and Crow tore out of the graveled lot in a thick cloud of dust.

"Let's just wait and see who found your bag." Crow turned onto the highway and headed back in the direction of the school. "But you have to realize, if there's any chance at all that your cover's been blown, you're out of there."

Angel sighed. He was right. It would be not only dangerous for her, but for Crow, as well, if her true identity were revealed.

Crow dropped her off in front of the school, and she raced up the front steps. The halls were filled with students, but Angel barely answered the few scattered greetings tossed her way. For once she was glad she didn't have many friends.

She wove her way through the students, praying that her bag would still be where she'd left it. The route was familiar and automatic, especially at this time of day. Her last class, history with Jake, was right across the hall from her locker.

By the time she got close, the halls were almost deserted and the warning bell had already rung. She had a clear view of the hall and the spot where she knew she'd left her bag.

Empty.

Her shoulders sagged.

Angel cast her eyes heavenward and sent up a silent plea. If given another chance, she knew she could solve this case. She wouldn't have accepted it if she'd thought otherwise.

The hair on the back of her neck stood up, and her hand automatically went to the side where she normally kept her weapon—then she remembered: she didn't have it with her.

"Angel," Jake called from the doorway behind her, and she whirled. His hand rose from his side, and dangling from his outstretched fingers hung her purple backpack.

He lifted a brow. "Looking for this?"

Angel tore her gaze from the bag, smiled with more than a bit of relief, and held out her hand. "Yep, it's mine. Hand it over."

"Got any proof?" He made no effort to let go of the backpack.

Frustrated, she let her arm drop to her side.

"What kind of proof?" She narrowed her gaze. "I said it was mine."

"Is there any identification in it showing it's yours?"

She stiffened. Had he found the license? Was he baiting her? She studied him carefully. Or was this teasing purely innocent?

"No ID," she said casually. "But I can identify every book that's in there."

"Okay, shoot."

"Shoot?"

"Name the textbooks."

She thought for a moment. "English Lit, Trig, your history book—"

"That's good enough." He held out the bag, and it was all she could do not to snatch it from his hands.

She hugged it to her chest, relieved to have it back in her possession. But something didn't feel quite right. How had *he* known the contents? "So, I take it you did look through it?"

He shrugged. "I glanced inside looking for a wallet, but there were only books."

She wanted to ask him why he'd made it sound like there was some sort of identification inside, but she didn't get the chance. The final bell sounded, and Jake motioned her toward the open classroom door. She entered in front of him.

He seemed sincere. Maybe this was her lucky day. Maybe she'd still have a chance to crack this case.

Or maybe she really had something to worry about.

Chapter Six

Jake dialed the number he'd been given and listened to the rings. *One. Two. Three.*

A woman answered just before the voice-mail kicked in. "Debra Dean."

"Ms. Dean. This is Jake Weston. I'm the assistant principal at Woodland Hills High School."

"What can I do for you, Mr. Weston?" The voice was businesslike but not unfriendly.

Jake took a deep breath and plunged ahead. "I'm trying to locate a friend who subbed for the district last semester. Unfortunately, our records at Woodland Hills are no help. He's no longer at his old address, and his phone has been disconnected."

"Hmm." She paused, and he could hear what

sounded like a pencil tapping against a desk. "I'm not sure if we'd have anything more current."

"Could you check?" It was all Jake could do to keep his tone even.

"I'm in the middle of something right now," she said. "Can I call you back?"

"Sure. Let me give you my number." He gave her his home, work and cellular numbers.

"I can't guarantee anything."

"I'll take whatever you have." Right now he had nothing. No current address or phone. No next of kin. Nothing.

"All right." She sighed. "Tell me what information you do have."

Jake answered her questions the best he could, which was hard considering he knew next to nothing about the guy.

He hoped that would soon change. By tomorrow he should have Tony's phone number. Then he'd know the extent of the relationship between the former teacher and Angel. And then he'd know what he needed to do.

Angel stood on the porch and stared at the ornate six-panel door. She glanced sideways and read the numbers etched in a stone block set in the brick. For the tenth time she verified that this home—this mansion—was indeed the site of the Woodland

Hills Community Church's monthly youth Bible study.

Emily's parents were hosting the event, and although her friend had invited her weeks ago, Angel hadn't planned to attend until Emily told her yesterday that Mike had changed his mind and decided to come after all. When Angel heard that Jake Weston would be substituting for the youth leader, wild horses couldn't keep her away.

But it wasn't just curiosity that brought her to this affluent suburban neighborhood. It was the fact that Jake would be in the same room with Mike and his friends. That fact seemed almost too coincidental.

Angel had initially scoffed when Crow had suggested that the youth group might be a front for drug activity, but she'd seen too many weird things in her years on the force to be so naive as to believe that something like that couldn't happen.

Angel had raised her hand to knock, when the door opened abruptly. "Hey, Em. What's up?"

Emily stopped, and her eyes widened in surprise. She quickly recovered and gave Angel a hug. "I'm so glad you could make it. I didn't think you were coming."

Angel shrugged, but she couldn't help but be pleased at the warm welcome. She'd alternately dreaded and looked forward to tonight's event. On the one hand, she couldn't wait to see how Jake would run the same type of youth meeting she herself ran before she'd gone undercover. On the other hand, she needed to stay in character tonight and remember she was here as a cop, first and foremost.

Emily directed her inside, and Angel moved off the front porch and into the foyer. She stopped, and her gaze lifted upward before dropping. It was hard to say which was more impressive: the two-story open entry or the Italian marble floor. The touch of an experienced interior designer was evident in the understated elegance that surrounded her.

"Nice place you got here," Angel said, snapping her gum. *Nice?* More like gorgeous.

Angel wiped her sweaty palms on the soft linen of her drawstring skirt, thankful she'd dressed up. The floral skirt and the scoop-necked T-shirt were trendy but appropriate for a church-sponsored event. Even her hair had cooperated. Normally the mass of wild curls stuck out from her face in every direction, but tonight at the last minute, she'd pulled the sides up and back, securing the strands with a couple of decorative clips.

"You look nice." Emily looped her arm through Angel's and gave it a squeeze. "It's wonderful to have a friend here."

The sincerity in Emily's voice touched Angel's heart. The fact that the girl could be so kind, so concerned about making Angel feel welcome when she herself was a nervous wreck was remarkable. Emily had been anxious about this Bible study all week, first worrying that no one would show up and then worrying, what if too many came and they ran out of food or space?

Angel had made like a good friend—voicing little reassurances and letting the girl talk endlessly about her concerns. But she'd only started really listening when Emily mentioned that Mike and his friends had decided to come.

They were almost at the end of the long hall when Emily's feet slowed. She stopped and turned. "Do you think I look okay?"

A wave of guilt washed over Angel. Here Emily had gone out of her way to make her feel comfortable, and yet she'd done nothing to assuage Emily's nervous anxiety.

"You look better than okay, Em. You look fabulous." Angel cast an approving look at the buttercup-yellow tank dress. Relaxed through the waist and hip, the dress minimized Emily's overly rounded curves.

Actually, tonight the girl looked svelte. Positively thin. Angel's gaze narrowed. "Have you lost weight?"

Emily flushed. "A little. I'd like to lose fifteen more."

A sick feeling took up residence in Angel's stomach. Had Emily succumbed to Mike's promise of easy weight loss with crank? Dear God, she hoped not. Angel lowered her voice to a whisper. "Tell me you haven't started—"

"What are you talking about?" Emily looked at her blankly, clearly puzzled.

"Using," Angel said tersely.

Awareness coupled with disappointment flickered across the girl's face. Her jaw clenched. "I thought you knew me better than that."

"Em." Angel grasped her arm. "I'm sorry. But if not that way, then how?"

"There are other ways to lose weight, besides drugs," Emily hissed. Her blue eyes flashed.

"Such as?" Angel hated to pry, but she had to know the score.

"Such as diet and exercise."

Angel raised a brow. "Really?"

"That's right." Emily brushed a strand of hair back from her face with a trembling hand. "My mom and I go work out together."

"You never said anything." Still, now that she thought about it, Emily *had* stopped eating those chocolate snack cakes in the afternoon, and Angel couldn't remember the last time the girl had drunk a shake with lunch.

"I didn't say anything because I wanted to see whether it worked or not," Emily said, the hurt still in her eyes. "I've lost ten pounds in a month."

"I'm really happy for you," Angel said. "And I'm really sorry for assuming the worst—but I know what Mike's been like. What's he got to say about all this, anyway?"

"Actually, I haven't seen much of him lately." Emily's gaze shifted to her hands and she bit at a cuticle. "He's been hanging out with his friends more."

"But didn't you say he's coming tonight?"

"That's what he said. But he can be sort of undependable." Emily frowned. "He's already changed his mind a couple of times. First he wasn't going to come, then he said he would."

"What made him decide?" Angel forced a teasing smile. "Missed you too much?"

An unladylike snort burst from Emily's lips. "Hardly. He found out Mr. Weston was doing the meeting."

"No way." Angel laughed. "So, he'd rather see the coach than you? Is that it?"

"I guess. I'm still trying to figure it all out." Emily shrugged, but Angel knew Mike's erratic behavior had upset the girl. Even though Mike was wrong for Emily, Angel hated to see her friend so unhappy. "We'd better go in."

Angel followed Emily into the oversize family room. Decorated in hunter green with brick-red accents, the massive room retained a homey feel. From the fireplace with its bouquet of spring flowers to the braided rug on the hardwood floor, the effect was warm and inviting.

For a second, though, when they walked in and all eyes shifted to the doorway, Angel felt more like Daniel entering the lion's den than a welcomed guest. At that moment, Emily wasn't the only one glad to have a friend at her side.

Angel scanned the crowd. She finally found Jake across the room, sandwiched among four students on a green-and-white striped sofa. Angel's gaze narrowed and she wished she were a fly on Jarvis Rediger's ball cap. She'd love to know what Jake was saying to the young outfielder.

"Hey, Angel." A boy she recognized from her Trig class yelled from the far corner of the room. "There's a seat over here by me."

Angel groaned. The guy had asked her out every day for the past month, and now she couldn't even remember his name.

She looked away to find Jake staring.

Their eyes locked. His lips turned up in a slight smile. Her heart skipped a beat. After promising to catch up with Emily later, Angel started across the room. She wove her way in and out among the casually arranged couches and chairs, keeping the striped sofa in sight.

"Why, Mr. Weston." She stopped beside the couch and widened her eyes innocently. "What a surprise."

Relief flashed across his face, and she almost wished she'd given in to her first impulse and called him "Jake, baby" or "Hey, sweetheart" or something equally outlandish, just to see his reaction.

"Good evening, Angel. I didn't expect to see you here. But," he added, "I didn't expect to see Jarvis, either."

Another student started talking to Jake, and Angel looked at Mike's best friend. Though they'd never been introduced, the guy his teammates had nicknamed "Big J" was well known around Woodland Hills High. His exploits were legendary. His parents were frequently out of town on business, and Jarvis used their absence to full advantage. His parties were reported to be "the best." Parties that—and she'd heard this from a reliable source—included an unending supply of crystal meth.

Did the boy use drugs to combat loneliness? Growing up, she'd been surrounded by kids who did just that. Or did he do it to fit in? Being a teen in today's world wasn't easy. It hadn't been easy when Angel was young, either. The path to adulthood was filled with temptations, especially when you were traveling it alone.

She smiled at Jarvis, er, Big J.

Jarvis returned her smile, showing a mouthful of perfect white teeth. He sat up straight, and his voice was husky and low. "Angel. At last we meet."

He stood, and for a crazy moment she thought he was going to kiss her hand. Instead he moved closer, forcing her to take a step back. "I've been watching you and I don't mind saying I like what I see. Tell me, are you and the boyfriend exclusive?" A hint of beer and tobacco clung to his breath, and her empty stomach churned.

"Boyfriend?" She raised an eyebrow.

"You know, the one with the tattoos. I see his car parked out in front of your place a lot."

Angel felt a cold wave of apprehension. The one constant in this suburban area was that most of those who lived in Woodland Hills never ventured across the tracks to the area Angel lived in—an area known as "Trashtown."

How did Jarvis know where she lived? And more important, how did he know when Crow was there? The thought that her house could be under surveillance had never occurred to her.

She decided to play dumb and see if he was bluffing. "Get real. You don't know where I live."

"Sure I do," he said with a wink. "I know where all the pretty girls sleep."

She ignored his emphasis on the word *sleep*. "Yeah, right. You're just making all this up."

"You live on Dempster, white house, middle of the block." Jarvis ran a finger down her bare arm, and it was all Angel could do not to slap it away. "I've seen you out in the yard in those hot shorts."

She rolled her eyes and folded her arms across her chest. "All right. You know where I live. So what are you doing in that neighborhood? I know you don't live around there."

He laughed as if she'd said something hilarious. "Me live in Trashtown? No way. But the guys and I do sometimes go over there and party. You know the place—the green house around the corner from you."

"The one on Gade?" Angel did know the place. She made a mental note to give Narcotics the address. "It has that washing machine on the front porch?"

"That's it." Jarvis shook his head. "Man, you missed a great party last week."

"You should have invited me." She gazed up at him through lowered lashes. "I like to party."

Jarvis leaned closer, and she held her breath. "I would have asked you, sweetheart, but I don't want your man to get all upset."

"I have an idea." She turned her face so her lips barely brushed his cheek and she whispered in his ear, "Let's not tell him."

"Angel." Jake had risen from his seat, and his voice, although abrupt and disapproving, was music to her ears. "You two can talk later. We're ready to get started."

Jarvis sat back in the oversize leather chair and patted his lap.

She forced a regret-filled smile, mouthed *sorry* and headed over to where Winston…? Kenneth…? from Trig waited.

"You can share my Bible." The tall Swede held up a leather-clad volume much like the one she'd left at home.

She'd thought about bringing hers, but, unfortunately, with her name embossed in gold across the front and her favorite passages well marked, the Book would be at odds with her wild Angel image.

It had been harder than she'd thought to keep her Christianity under wraps. For the past ten years, sharing her faith—letting her light shine—had been as much a part of her life as breathing.

Thanks to her old friend Dan Reilly.

Dan had been working the streets in East St. Louis that long ago night when her uncle had forced Angel to accompany him on that fateful drug buy. One of the first officers to respond to the report of shots fired, Dan had told her later that when she'd looked up at him from that pool of blood and cried for help, there wasn't anything he wouldn't have done for her.

Wounded and in shock, Angel only remembered bits and pieces of the evening. But she did know Dan had been there when she'd awakened and he'd been by her side ever since.

With his wife dead and his only son grown and living out of state, Dan had in abundance what Angel needed most: time and love. He became her surrogate father and although they were both too strong willed to always agree, she and the burly police officer shared a special bond. He was her hero, her mentor and most of all, her friend.

It was through his quiet witnessing that she'd come to faith. She knew firsthand the power of true Christian caring.

She smiled to herself and sent up her daily prayer of thanks to God for bringing that man into her life.

Her Trig partner nudged her, and she realized that everyone but Jarvis and her had bowed their head in prayer.

Angel folded her hands and shifted her gaze to where Jake now stood in front of the fireplace. His words were strong and clear, and the opening prayer he'd chosen touched her heart. It was so hard to believe the man could be the head of a methamphetamine ring. But she remembered one of her first arrests: a sweet old grandmother who raised marijuana in her basement to supplement her Social Security. Nothing, Angel reminded herself, was impossible.

"Tonight, we're going to discuss Matthew 14:2 'Come, He said.'" Jake rested one hand on the mantel and waited for everyone to locate the passage. "But before we get started, I'm going to ask Marylou Dettoff to come to the front of the room."

The sound of thin pages flipping filled the room as the plump blonde made her way toward the fireplace.

Winston?—Kenneth?—found the text immediately, and his face lit with pleasure. Though he sometimes came across as trying way too hard, he seemed like a genuinely nice guy. Angel gave him an approving smile. A splotch of red darkened his neck. The Book slipped from his hand.

Angel grabbed it before it hit the floor.

"I'm sor—"

"I'm sor—"

He chuckled and Angel giggled.

Jake watched the two in silence. He was glad Angel had made friends with Ken. The boy was relatively new to Woodland Hills, and for some reason was having difficulty fitting in. Kids could be so cruel. An unwanted image of two boys in shackles rose unbidden in Jake's mind. He shoved the memory aside and tried to listen to Marylou's solo.

Why had he agreed to do this? The question went round and round in his head. Granted, the youth director had made a special plea, and Jerry was hard to resist. But, Jake reminded himself, he'd said no for almost a year. Why had he said yes now?

Jim's death had rocked his faith, but despite what Amanda thought, it was too much of who he was for him to abandon it without a backward glance. But did this mean he was ready to forgive those who had committed such a horrible act? His chest tightened and a familiar tight knot of hate welled up from deep inside. No, he would never forgive them. *Never.*

Marylou concluded her rendition of an old Amy Grant tune with a bow, a broad smile lighting her features. Jake added his applause to the others and gave her a quick thumbs-up as she passed by on her way to her seat. He glanced around the room, surveying the crowd. Most of those in attendance tonight were regulars who'd been coming since they'd started high school.

Emily and Ken were new, as were Jarvis and Mike—who'd just slipped in and was whispering feverishly to his friend. Jake silenced him with a stare before his gaze shifted momentarily to Angel.

She smiled, and to his chagrin he immediately looked away, behaving in that instant not much differently than some of the young boys he coached.

Emily moved to take a place at his side. "Now?" she whispered.

He nodded, and Emily punched a button on the remote.

A loud *crack* of thunder rent the air. A few kids jumped. Some girls giggled.

Satisfied, Jake smiled. Now that he'd captured their attention, he needed to make the most of it. He proceeded like a master storyteller—his voice dramatic and loud one minute, hushed the next, as he set the scene.

"You're out on a lake, and a storm blows in. Unable to handle the fierce wind and rain, your boat capsizes and you're suddenly thrown into the cold dark water. You panic. Your life jacket is in the boat, and you're too far from shore to swim. You're drowning,'' Jake said. ''The water is pulling you down. You don't know how much longer you can go on.''

He paused. ''Who or what would you want to see most at that moment?''

''A lifeguard in a bikini!'' Mike shouted out.

''Flipper,'' Marylou said.

''My dad in his speedboat,'' Kenneth yelled.

The answers continued coming fast and furiously for several moments.

''Lots of good ideas.'' Jake rubbed his hands together and paced the room, moving in and out among the students as the adrenaline flowed. ''Now, let's take this back to our lesson for the evening.''

He returned to his original spot by the fireplace and read the passage aloud. ''Do you ever feel like the person in the example? That you're drowning and you're all alone? We don't have to be in water to feel like we're going under or being pulled down. Give me some examples of times you've had that same feeling.''

''When I sit down in the lunchroom and everyone gets up and moves.'' The words rushed from Kenneth's mouth before he clamped it shut, as if realizing too late what he'd said. To Jake's surprise, Angel slipped an arm around the boy's shoulders and gave him a hug.

"When someone pressures me to do something I know I shouldn't." Emily cast a pointed glance at Mike.

"What can we as Christians do in such situations?" The room, which only moments ago had been filled with laughter and youthful voices, hung silent. "C'mon people, this isn't that hard."

"We can reach out a helping hand." This time it was Angel who answered. "We can live our faith and do as Christ would do."

Jake stared, taken aback. It was the answer he'd hoped for, but he'd never expected it to come from Angel. "Exactly right," he said. "Let's turn back to the text and talk about how as Christians we should be there for each other, and above all, how God is always there for us. So that in our darkest moments we're never alone."

As Jake moderated the discussion, he suddenly realized he'd spent the past year trying to make it through Jim's death on his own. Although his pastor and others had tried to help him, he'd shoved them aside. And after a while they'd done as he'd asked and left him alone. But the One who'd been there since the beginning had never left.

"We all need to remember," Jake said, "when

we start to go under, to feel overwhelmed, all we have to do is reach out and take Jesus's hand.''

The students stared silently at him. Jake could only hope that at least a few had gotten the message tonight. *He* certainly had.

''Would anyone like to share an example from their own life?''

Granted, it was a large group, and high school students were into appearing cool, but Jake had expected at least two or three to volunteer. No one did. He was just about ready to give a general example when Angel spoke.

''Several years ago, I was down so low I couldn't see how I could ever get out. My friends were no help. They were as messed up as I was. Then I met someone who turned me on to Christ and—'' Angel's voice faltered for a second. ''I found out like Peter that if I keep my eyes focused on Christ, I can not only always keep my head above water but I can actually swim a few strokes.''

The familiar brashness returned to her eyes. ''I must admit, I still have my moments of weakness. But that's another story.''

Everyone laughed, and Jake couldn't help but join in.

''Thanks for sharing, Angel.'' Jake resumed control of the meeting, answered a few questions and then closed with a simple prayer. "Walk with us, Jesus. All the way. Every day. Amen."

With the conclusion of the Bible study, the social hour began.

Emily's mother brought out platters of desserts to supplement the huge bowls of popcorn mixed with pretzels and M&Ms.

A few minutes later, Jake made his way across the crowded room to Angel. He cupped her elbow in his hand. "I really appreciated your comments."

"Don't read too much into it," she said with a wink. "I'll do anything to get center stage."

Jake narrowed his gaze. Was she saying it had all been a big joke? Was this Christian thing just that? An act? Another lie?

"Okay, now that makes sense," Jarvis spoke up, and Jake realized the boy had been standing behind him. "For a moment I wondered if I'd had too much—er, Pepsi—to drink. It just didn't sound like you, Angel, babe. Unless, of course, you and your biker man are talkin' religion when he's over there shacking up."

Jake's gaze jerked to Angel. The look she shot Jarvis could have melted steel.

"Crow helps me with my homework," she said.

"I didn't know Anatomy was offered this semester," Jarvis said with a sly smile.

"He lends her a helping hand," Mike answered, and the boys both laughed.

"That's enough," Jake said sharply. "Any more of that kind of talk and you'll have to leave."

"Sorry." Mike sounded not at all contrite.

"Me, too." Jarvis made a show of wiping the smile from his lips. "We were just joking. Angel knew that. Didn't you, Angel?"

Jake didn't give her a chance to answer. He fixed a gaze on the boys. "Remember what I said. Keep it clean or you're out of here."

For the next hour, Jake mingled with the students, spent time talking with Emily's parents and watched Angel out of the corner of his eye.

He couldn't believe she was twenty-six. She looked more like an eighteen-year-old than half the girls in the room did tonight. In fact, she didn't look a lot different than she had in that picture.

Dear Lord, please help me find Tony D'Fusco.

It seemed a selfish prayer, and he felt guilty for even sending it heavenward. Although he could say it was because he needed to know her identity for the good of the students and the school, deep down he knew it had little to do with Woodland Hills High, and a whole lot more to do with how she made him feel.

"She's pretty, isn't she," Emily's mother said suddenly.

"Who?" Jake turned to her. He took a sip of tea.

"Angel." Anne Weyer lowered her voice. "Oh, I'll grant you, the first time I met her I had my reservations."

"But now?"

"I like her," she said simply. "She's been good for Emily. And she's a classic example of looks being deceiving."

Deceiving.

"You think so?" He cast another glance at Angel, wondering what she was up to, not liking how close she stood to Jarvis. Or rather, how close the boy stood to her.

"She's a young woman who's got her head on straight, despite her rather unconventional appearance." Anne laughed. "But you have to understand, the first time I met Joe he had a ponytail."

Jake couldn't imagine Joe Weyer, an investment banker, with hair longer than a quarter inch. Jake's gaze slipped to the beverage table, where Emily's dad was dispensing sodas and juice. It was a good thing Joe'd had it while he still could. Now, what hair he had left hung in thin wispy strands across a shiny dome.

Jake shook his head and turned back to Anne. "Does Angel spend a lot of time at your house?"

"Tonight's the first time she's been here. We've invited her before but she's always said no." Anne's gaze shifted to Angel and her expression grew thoughtful. "The three of us go to lunch on the weekends, and occasionally she'll go with Emily and me to an art exhibit or concert. I think she's lonely."

"What about Crow?" The question on Jake's mind slipped from his lips. "Does he ever come, too?"

"I've never met him, and to tell you the truth I'm not sure what's going on there." She paused and worry lines appeared between her brows. "She's fond of him, but...I don't know...it's a strange relationship."

"Do you think they're...intimate?" The question had troubled him since he'd first seen them together in the park, but he'd certainly never meant to voice it. He glanced at the red plastic cup in his hand, supposedly filled with iced tea. Unless good old Joe had spiked the beverage, Jake had no good excuse for asking the question.

Surprisingly, Anne didn't seem to find it out of line. With a start, Jake realized that despite their age difference, Emily's mother considered him to be her peer rather than her daughter's. "I couldn't say, but from what Emily tells me, I doubt it. Now, let me ask you a question. What do think of that boy over there with my daughter?" Ann gestured with her head to the blond boy standing across the room with his arm around Emily.

"Mike Blaine?" Jake paused and thought for a minute. "Good athlete. Comes from a nice family."

"Is that all?"

With a start, Jake realized that was all he knew. He'd coached the boy since he was a freshman but he really didn't know much about Mike. The kid was cocky—no one would argue that—but he followed directions and had never really given Jake any trouble.

Right now, he stood with his arm looped around Emily's shoulder, blatantly ignoring her father's disapproving gaze.

"I don't like him and I sure don't trust him." Anne gathered up some discarded plates, her voice so low that Jake had to strain to hear. "Mark my words, that boy's headed for trouble."

Jake wanted to tell her that Big J was the one headed for trouble. The boy was a predator, a seducer of females who'd gained his nickname from doing more than holding hands.

And right now Loverboy had Angel trapped, his hands flat against the wall on both sides of her body, pinning her in.

No, Mrs. Weyer didn't trust Mike, and Jake didn't trust Jarvis. Not one bit. And he was going to do something about it. He headed across the room.

Chapter Seven

Tom Jorgens rapped lightly on the door and shifted from one foot to the other. A warm breeze ruffled his hair and the familiar scent of lilacs tickled his nose.

Jane had loved lilacs.

Her casket had been covered in lilacs.

The thought brought a dull pain, and made the faint sounds of laughter and conversation filtering through the door unpalatable. The company of others held no appeal. There was only one thing that made him feel good. Only one thing he needed. And he wasn't going to let anyone or anything take away that one pleasure.

The door opened abruptly.

Tom jumped. The nerves in his skin fired along the surface like a semiautomatic weapon.

"Why, Mr. Jorgens." Emily Weyer's mouth dropped open. She shut it with a snap. "Hello. My father said he thought he heard someone drive up." The girl opened the door wider. "Come on in. We just finished with the Bible study."

No wonder Emily looked so surprised. He'd never made any bones about his religious beliefs. God, he'd decided long ago, simply didn't exist, and those who believed otherwise were engaged in wishful thinking.

Tom realized Emily was staring. The question she wouldn't ask shone strong in her blue eyes. He cursed his own stupidity. Why hadn't he taken the time to think of a plausible explanation as to why he'd stopped by?

He smiled and frantically searched for an excuse, a believable lie. But nothing would come when he had so much other stuff weighing heavily on his mind.

"From the cars outside, looks like you got a good turnout," Tom said with feigned interest.

"Almost fifty," Emily said proudly. "The only bad thing about the whole deal is that since most kids didn't carpool, all the on-street parking is gone. My dad said he hopes the neighbors don't call the cops and complain."

Cops.

Tom thought of the tip he'd received from a "friend" late this afternoon. It couldn't be true. They'd been too careful.

"Mr. Jorgens? Are you okay?" Emily touched his arm, her eyes filled with concern.

No, I'm not okay, he wanted to scream. One wrong careless move could bury him. He had to speak with Mike…to warn him.

"I'm fine." He forced a reassuring smile. "It was just a busy day at school."

"I'm sure being a principal is hard. You must have to deal with one problem after another."

"Sometimes it seems that way." Problems like—had they placed another cop in his school? Jake Weston said no, but then, he might be in on it with them.

"You look tired." The girl's voice was soft and gentle.

Tom rubbed the bridge of his nose with two fingers and blinked. "I am tired. I just need to talk to Mr. Weston for a minute, then I'm headed home."

Why he'd mentioned Jake Weston, he didn't know. But the more he thought about it, the more it seemed like a good idea.

Emily gestured to an open doorway at the end of the hall. "He's in the family room. We're all just hanging out." She glanced to the right. "I was going to get some more iced tea...."

Tom waved a dismissive hand. "Go and get your tea. I think I can find my way to the end of the hall. Of course, I'll yell if I get lost."

Emily giggled. Her nose scrunched up and her blue eyes sparkled. What would it have been like if he and Jane had been able to have children? What if he'd had a daughter like Emily? She would have brought noise to his silent house and love to his empty life. Maybe then he wouldn't be so lonely. He might not have needed something else to keep him going. But then again—Tom brushed aside the sentimental ramblings—maybe it wouldn't.

He stopped at the arched doorway and his gaze scanned the crowd until he located Mike Blaine.

Lately Tom had found himself wishing he'd never gotten involved with the kid in the first place. Teenagers could be so unpredictable.

Keeping Mike in sight, Tom started across the room. He hadn't gone ten feet before he ran into his "excuse." "Jake, just the man I wanted to see."

Jake's eyes widened. "Tom, what a surprise. You're the last person I expected to see here."

"I was in the neighborhood." Two years of continual lies had made Tom a master. "I saw your

Jeep and thought I'd stop by. There's something I need to discuss with you.''

"It must be important if it couldn't wait until tomorrow." Jake's expression turned serious.

"I'm going to be out of the office the rest of the week and it *is* important." Tom pulled Jake aside and lowered his voice. "It's something I didn't want to discuss at school, anyway. You never know who might be listening."

"What is it?" Jake's voice conveyed concern.

"I think the police were right." Tom spoke in a conspiratorial whisper. If he could pull this off, he'd deserve an Oscar. "I now believe one of our teachers *is* involved in that drug ring."

"What made you change your mind?"

"The police." Tom met Jake's gaze, grateful that at least this part of the story was true. "They called and asked for a list of all the subs we've used since September."

Jake's brows drew together in a thoughtful frown. "So they think the person they're looking for is a sub?"

Tom hid a smile. This latest police wild-goose chase couldn't have come at a better time. Shifting suspicion to the temporary staff might be his salvation. "It looks that way."

"But what does this have to do with me?"

Tom tried to keep the exasperation from his

voice. "The police want those names by five o'clock Monday. I want you to get that list together."

Jake shook his head. "I'd like to help, Tom, but I think you'd be better off checking with the central office. They should have that information in their computer system."

"You'd think so," Tom said. "But when the administration converted to that new system at the end of December, they erased a bunch of files and they say they don't have them. That's where you come in."

"Me?" Jake raised both hands and took a step back. "I know I've done some special projects, but I'm afraid retrieving lost files—especially ones that have been erased—are beyond my expertise."

Tom shook his head. "Forget the computer. Just start making a list of the names of any subs you remember."

When Jake hesitated, Tom forced a hint of pleading into his voice, pleased when it came out just as he'd intended. "Everyone knows you've got a mind like a steel trap. You never forget a name. I'd consider it a personal favor, Jake. If there's someone doing this kind of stuff in my school, I want them caught. And the sooner the better."

"I hear you, Tom." Jake clasped the man's shoulder. "You can count on me."

"I still don't see why you came here tonight." Mike's gaze darted from side to side as if he were making sure no one was in listening distance.

"Because, you fool—" the principal spoke through gritted teeth but, to Mike's amazement, still managed to smile and wave at Emily's mother across the room "—I needed to let you know to steer clear of that house on Gade. Word is the cops are watching it. And us."

Mike glanced over to where Emily stood talking to Kenneth Hurlburt. He didn't like the way she smiled up at the geek. That was the very reason he'd come to this thing tonight—to keep her away from those straight-as-an-arrow religious types.

Emily didn't realize how pretty she was or how desirable. Initially the other guys hadn't taken much notice of her, but lately that had changed. Look at Kenneth: he was practically drooling.

"Are you even listening to me?"

Mike turned his attention back to Tom, but didn't even try to hide his irritation. Lately, the man had been getting on his nerves. "You could have just called. Or paged me."

"Too dangerous." Tom shook his head. "Calls can be traced…intercepted."

"You know..." With great effort Mike reined in his rising temper. "You're sounding super paranoid. It's a real drag."

Tom's eyes hardened and Mike cursed his foolishness. The guy was strung tighter than a guitar string, and it wouldn't take much to set him off.

"Okay, okay," Mike said soothingly. "Thanks for the warning. I appreciate it."

"You'll steer clear of the place?" The principal's chest rose and fell as if he'd been running a race.

"You bet." Mike stared at the man. Some people could handle crank. This one obviously couldn't. "Thanks for letting me know, man."

"Know what?" Angel asked softly behind him.

They both jumped. Mike forced a chuckle. "Don't good angels know they shouldn't listen to other people's conversations?"

"The key word there is *good*." She smiled. "I'm curious as a cat. So what were you two whispering about? I can keep secrets. I promise."

Mike thought quickly. It was obvious from Tom's silence that he wasn't going to be of any help. "Mr. Jorgens was telling me he'd heard that I was going to be named to the Super State team again. But—" Mike touched a finger to his lips and lowered his voice "—it's not official yet, so we have to keep it quiet."

Angel's smile widened. "Congratulations. You must be thrilled."

"Yeah, thrilled." If he could get rid of Tom he'd be thrilled. Mike looked over Angel's shoulder at Emily and Kenneth, now sitting side by side on a floral love seat. His jaw clenched. Next thing you know, the guy would have his arm around her.

Over my dead body.

"Hey, it's been great but I gotta go. Thanks again, Mr. Jorgens, for the news."

The two watched the boy make a beeline across the room to join Emily and Kenneth on the sofa.

"He's quite a guy," said Angel.

"Yes, he is."

"That's great about the Super State thing," Angel said.

"Super State?" The principal paused, then nodded. "Oh, yes. I couldn't wait to tell him."

Angel lingered at the door. Everyone else had gone but she'd stayed behind to help clean up. Emily's mother had told her the maid was more than capable of handling it, but Angel had insisted. And for good reason. She needed to find out what was going on.

"I had a great time tonight, Em."

A satisfied smile tipped the corner of Emily's

lips. "It went better than I ever could have hoped."

"Mike seemed all about you tonight." Angel tossed the words out casually and watched for the girl's reaction.

"I know." A rosy flush dotted Emily's cheeks. "He came over when I was talking to Kenneth, and for a second I thought he was…well, jealous."

"Of Kenneth?" Despite the fact she'd gotten the same impression, Angel couldn't quite keep the incredulity from her voice.

"I know Kenneth isn't as good-looking as Mike, but he's a nice guy." Emily's eyes flashed.

Angel raised her hands in mock surrender. "Hey, I didn't mean anything by it. Honest."

Emily scuffed her toe into the deep plush of the carpet, her eyes downcast. "Kenneth is sweet, and I don't want you or anyone else dogging him."

Angel touched Emily's arm. "I like him, too, Em. And if it sounded like I was saying anything against him, I'm sorry."

The smile Emily shot her was wobbly, but it was laced with forgiveness, and Angel couldn't ask for more.

"Mike and Jarvis sure took off suddenly." Angel pasted a concerned expression on her face. "I hope nothing was wrong."

Emily snorted, and the look in her eyes told Angel that Mike hadn't scored any brownie points tonight.

"He got a page," Emily said. She shook her head in disgust. "I swear his friends mean more to him than anything...or anyone."

Ah, so that's how it is, Angel thought. Not only had Kenneth been pleasant and attentive, but Mike had fallen short. He'd let his "business dealings" interfere with his love life, even though it had been obvious tonight how much he liked Emily. Angel had never felt that Mike was right for Emily, but she felt almost sorry for the guy. He just kept making the wrong choices.

"Maybe his parents were sick. Maybe that's why he had to leave so suddenly."

"And maybe I'm Miss America." Emily rolled her eyes. "Give me a break, Angel. You know as well as I do, it has something to do with drugs."

Angel forced herself to go slow. "He's really into the stuff, huh?"

"Let's go outside." Emily gestured with her head up the stairs. "You never know who might be listening."

They stepped out onto the porch, and Emily pulled the door shut behind her. She sat on the front step and Angel joined her.

"You're right." A deep resignation ran through Emily's voice. "He is really into the stuff. And even though I like him, I'm not sure I still want to see him.''

Personally, Angel applauded the girl's decision; professionally, she didn't want the relationship to end. Not just yet. If the two quit dating, her pipeline to information would dry up. Still, nothing was more important than Emily's safety.

''Does he ever use when he's with you?'' Angel stared at the ornate light pole at the end of the drive. She thought of all the kids she'd hung out with when she'd really been in high school—the ones who'd spent their days and nights strung out on one thing or another. Now most of them were dead. Or in prison.

''No. He never has.'' Emily rested her chin on her hand and sighed. ''He talks about it a lot. Keeps telling me he knows I'd like it if I'd just give it a try.''

''And what do you tell him when he puts on the pressure?''

''That it's not for me. But he sure is persistent. In some strange way I think he feels if I do it, too, that means it's okay that he does it.'' Emily shook her head. ''I know it sounds weird, but I really think it's important to him that I think what he's doing is right. It sounds paranoid, but I'm afraid he'll try to give me some stuff without me knowing.''

Angel swallowed hard. "I used to have friends that would bake brownies with pot in them or slip LSD in open cans of soda. I got so I wouldn't drink out of an already opened can or eat at any of their parties."

"That's smart." Emily sighed. "But then again, what's smart about hanging out with druggies? Tonight I started asking myself, why am I doing this? Why am I putting myself in this type of situation? Is this what God would want me to do?"

Angel knew the answer as well as Emily did.

"Maybe Mike's trying to change," Angel said, not answering Emily's question. "He came to Bible study tonight, didn't he?"

"He might have been in the room, but I doubt he got anything out of the lesson. He and Jarvis spent most of the evening laughing and talking." Emily shook her head. "To tell you the truth, I'm not sure why he came."

"Didn't you say you thought it was because Jake, er, Mr. Weston came?"

"That's what I thought."

"But now?"

"I'm not so sure." Emily reached back and massaged her neck with one hand. "They hardly talked to each other, and Mr. Weston seemed as surprised as anyone that Mike was here."

Angel agreed. She'd watched Jake out of the

corner of her eye all evening and there was no indication that the boys came to meet with him. Actually, Mike had spent more time talking to the principal than he had to Jake.

That was something else that didn't make any sense. Why would a man who professed to be an agnostic show up at a Bible study? "What was the deal with Mr. Jorgens? Why did he come by?"

Emily shrugged. "Beats me. He told my mother he was just in the neighborhood. But he told me he had something to discuss with Mr. Weston."

Tom Jorgens.

Mike Blaine.

Jake Weston.

Was there a connection? Were the pieces finally starting to fall into place?

Angel jumped to her feet and bid Emily a hasty goodbye. She couldn't wait to call Crow.

Chapter Eight

The night sky was clear and the lights from the midway sparkled like brightly colored jewels. The aroma of buttered popcorn filled the air.

Angel inhaled deeply, and a shiver of excitement raced through her. Not only was she at a carnival, she was here with him! She glanced at Jake walking by her side. Dressed casually in a blue cotton polo and a pair of khaki shorts, the guy looked more like a *GQ* model than a history teacher.

She'd been following him for the past couple of days. Running into him at the entrance to the carnival had been no accident, but getting him to agree to accompany her on a walk through the midway had been a stroke of genius.

They were far enough from Woodland Hills that

they shouldn't run into anyone they knew. How could it get much better?

If only she didn't feel so jittery. Her insides bounced around as if she'd swallowed a handful of those Mexican jumping beans she'd had as a child.

But she wasn't a child; she was an adult. An adult who now regretted not eating lunch. She jumped on the excuse and decided that must be the reason she felt so shaky. Angel took a deep breath and slipped her arm through his. "I'm dying for some cotton candy. How 'bout you?"

An expression of unease crossed his handsome face, but to her surprise he didn't pull his arm away. "Sure."

They stopped in front of a stand with bags of pink and blue fluff suspended from the ceiling. A huge tub was in constant rotation, spinning the sweet treat right before their eyes.

Angel reminded herself that she needed to play this cool, to be natural. She leaned over the counter and pointed to the tub. "I want the fresh stuff."

Jake chuckled and laid a couple of bills on the shiny metal counter. "Make that two."

The woman swirled the spun sugar onto paper cones and handed them each one.

Angel pulled off a huge chunk and popped the

entire piece into her mouth. She smiled at Jake. "Thanks."

"No problem." His gaze lingered on her lips. Her heart picked up speed and an odd fluttering gripped her belly.

Jake took a step closer. His head lowered. She lifted her face.

"Angie!" A shrill voice yelled above the crowd's noise. *"Over here."*

Angel stiffened. She immediately took a step back.

Jake stared, his green eyes a dark jade. "She said 'Angie,' not 'Angel.'"

"I know." Angel ignored the pounding in her chest. What had made her move back just as he was getting close?

"Does it bother you that I'm a teacher?" he asked, his expression impassive.

A part of her that had nothing to do with the investigation wanted to scream, *"Yes. I'm a student. No matter how much you like me, it's not right."*

Instead she swallowed the words and her disappointment and forced a smile. "If it bothered me, I wouldn't be here."

A tiny smile played at the corners of Jake's lips. "Good."

Good? What had gotten into the man? Ever

since she'd arrived at Woodland Hills High School, he'd maintained his distance. Now, all of a sudden, he seemed to have cast all inhibitions aside. It didn't make any sense, and that in itself sent up a red flag.

"I'm glad you decided to get over your hang-up about younger women." The minute the words left her mouth she would have given anything to take them back. Had she gone crazy? What was she trying to do? Push him away?

But again Jake surprised her. He laughed. "You're not a typical eighteen-year-old."

Her breath caught in her throat. "I'm not?"

"No." He took her elbow and propelled her down the dusty aisle between food vendors. "You're mature for your age. Remember?"

"Ya think so?" Angel turned, and suddenly they were face to face, so close she could feel the beating of his heart.

"Yeah, I'm sure of it."

Sure? He was sure of it? He thought she was eighteen. How could he possibly think this was right?

"Where do we go from here?" Her voice came out as a husky whisper, giving no clue to her tangled emotions.

His smile widened to a grin, and he stepped back

and pointed to the sky. "I don't think we have anywhere to go but up."

She lifted her gaze. The biggest Ferris wheel she'd ever seen towered above them. It lit up the sky. "It's huge."

"It's a double one. They're the best," he said with the authority of one who knows his Ferris wheels. "You're not afraid of heights, are you?"

Excitement surged. When she was little there had never been enough money for fairs or carnivals...or Ferris wheels.

"You aren't, are you?" He sounded worried, and she wondered which of them would be the most disappointed if she said yes.

"Me?" She lifted her chin, shoved her fears aside and flashed him a cocky grin. "I'm not afraid of anything."

It wasn't bad going up, but her stomach rose to her throat each time the big wheel began its downward spin. It was only bearable when she scrunched her eyes shut and clutched Jake's arm.

"Having fun?"

They were on their way up again. Angel opened her eyes and loosened her death grip. "It's great."

"Are you sure?" His eyes were filled with concern instead of the teasing glint that she'd expected. "For a moment there, you looked a little green."

She swallowed her breakfast for the second time. "No, really. I'm fine."

They slowly ascended, and Angel took advantage of the opportunity to keep her eyes open. The view was spectacular. The lights of the carnival lay before them, spread out in all directions. The people below appeared small and insignificant, and heaven above within reach.

A light breeze fanned Angel's cheek, and for the first time since she'd run into Jake, she relaxed.

She turned to tell him she thought she was getting the hang of it, just as the big wheel emitted a loud groan. It jerked to a stop. Their car swung wildly.

Jake's arm slipped protectively around her shoulder, and he pulled her close.

"What happened?" She tried to keep the panic from her voice.

"I think—" he peered over the edge "—that we're broken down."

Lightheaded, Angel closed her eyes and exhaled a loud breath.

"It'll be okay." His arm tightened around her. "They'll have it fixed in no time."

Without opening her eyes, Angel rested her head back against his arm. "Just give me a minute."

"I thought you said heights didn't bother you." His voice was low and teasing.

It was obvious he was trying to distract her, and even though it didn't work she still appreciated his efforts.

Angel opened her eyes but kept her gaze firmly fixed on his face. She refused to look down. For now her world would be this little compartment—and Jake Weston. "It might be hard to believe, but I've never been this high before."

"No way." He tilted his head, clearly skeptical. "What about in a plane?"

"I've never flown."

"You're kidding."

He was just making conversation so there really was no need to be honest, but for some reason she answered truthfully. "No. In fact, I've never even been out of the state."

"Now I know you're putting me on."

"I wish I were." She remembered all the places she'd read about. "I used to dream about traveling to faraway places. For years I dreamed of Hawaii. I'd imagine myself wearing a grass skirt, climbing a volcano or lounging on the beach. I could smell the ocean and feel the sand between my toes. It's almost laughable."

"Why was it laughable?" His gaze was puzzled. "Lots of people go to Hawaii."

"Not those who live in East St. Louis." Now *there* was a place she remembered all too vividly.

She only needed to close her eyes to be there again, to see the garbage-strewn streets, the buildings that hadn't seen a paintbrush in years, the gangs on the corners. She kept her eyes wide open. "It's hard enough just to survive."

"I didn't know you'd lived there. What was it like?"

"Picture hell on earth." She couldn't think of a better way to describe it. "Why?"

For a moment, Jake stared at his hands and didn't answer. When he finally spoke, the strain in his voice matched the tightness in his jaw. "My brother taught at a high school in East St. Louis. He…was killed by some punks that he'd tried to befriend. You might even know them."

Angel didn't ask their names. "I'm sorry about your brother. I can't even begin to imagine how hard that must have been."

He chuckled but there was no humor in the sound. "It was God's will."

"Who says?"

"Everyone."

"Well, not me."

"That's right," he said. "You don't believe."

Angel frowned as much in confusion as in reaction to the bitterness in his voice. "What are you talking about?"

"At the Bible study, you said you didn't believe."

Her spine stiffened. She'd never denied her faith. "I never said that."

"You implied it."

"Whatever." For an instant she forgot where she was and scooted across the seat, trying to put some distance between them. The car shifted with the sudden movement, and automatically Angel's gaze dropped. Her eyes widened and her stomach pitched.

Firm gentle hands pulled her back.

"Look at me," he ordered in his no-nonsense teacher voice. "Take a deep breath."

Her gaze rose. For what seemed an eternity, they breathed in and out together until her panic subsided.

"I'm okay now."

"Good." He tenderly brushed back a strand of hair from her face, then pulled her close, pressing her head to his chest. "There's nothing for you to be afraid of, Angel. I won't let anything happen to you."

Angel wanted to tell him she didn't need his protection. For years she'd dodged bullets and knives and fists and had always come out on top. Crow called her a survivor, jokingly telling the other cops that she was one woman who didn't need a man.

It was true. Physically, she could hold her own. Emotionally, she'd always been able to keep her distance.

Until she'd met Jake Weston. From the first time she'd seen the teacher, it had been different.

Teacher.

Angel froze. She wanted nothing more than to push him away and tell him to remember she was a student. *His* student. But she couldn't. She had too important a role to play. Her only concession was to lift her head from its comfortable position against his chest and swivel in his arms to meet his gaze head-on. "You don't need to worry about me. I can take care of myself."

"You know my brother said something like that to me once." Jake looked at her for what felt like a long time. "The next week he was dead."

A chill that had nothing to do with the increasing breeze from the north swept through her. Had Jake turned to drugs as a way to deal with the loss? "Tell me about him."

He paused, and she waited for him to tell her to mind her own business. But he didn't. He took a deep breath, and the words came slow and halting. "Jim was…great. Everyone liked him. He had this way of bringing out the best in people."

His voice caught, and he shifted in the seat, his arm moving to his side. Angel knew it was her cue to move. Instead she scooted even closer. Her finger traced a pattern across the front of his shirt, and she kept her gaze low.

"What happened?"

"His apartment was burglarized. He came back while they were still there. They killed him." Jake recited the events matter-of-factly. He could have been talking about a stranger rather than his own brother.

But his breath came in shallow puffs and the muscles in his arm were strung tight.

"I'm sorry, Jake."

"Yeah, well, me too."

"Was your brother a Christian?"

His gaze jerked back to her and his eyes narrowed. "Why do you ask?"

Angel didn't flinch. "Was he?"

"Yes," Jake said at last. "He was."

"I'm so glad." She heaved a relieved sigh. "At least you know he's with God."

"If there is a God."

"Jake." Angel whirled in the seat to face him. "You don't mean that."

"What if I do?" His jaw tightened defiantly. "There're a lot of people who don't believe."

"But you're not one of them."

"You're right." His voice was barely audible. "I can't deny my faith any longer. But I can't understand why Jim had to die, either."

Angel paused. Despite his simple words, despite his doubt, she knew his faith was as much a part of him as those infectious dimples. It ran through him like a deep and abiding river. She'd sensed it at Bible study. And she sensed it now.

"I don't know why your brother's life was cut short. I'm not going to say it's because God must have really wanted him. Sometimes things just happen." Angel slipped her arm across his chest, hoping he would find some comfort in the simple closeness.

"It's hard," he said. "I thought he'd pull through. I never got a chance to tell him I loved him. Or even to say how proud I was of him."

"He knew."

"I don't know." Jake sighed and turned away. "What does it matter, anyway?"

But Angel knew it did matter. A lot. "Did your brother love you?"

"Of course he did."

"How do you know? Did he tell you?"

"Of course not. I just kn—" Jake stopped, and she could see him ponder what he'd been about to say. Finally he nodded. "You're right. He knew how I felt."

Angel smiled. "I knew you were a smart guy."

"Did you?" His voice was low and husky.

She shivered. Throwing caution overboard, she leaned closer. "You know what else?"

His eyes darkened again to a smoky jade. "What?"

"I want to kiss you." She ignored her own good sense and pressed her lips to his. They were just as she'd imagined. Soft. Warm. Wonderful.

For a second he didn't respond, and it appeared that her bliss would be short-lived. Then his arms tightened about her, and he answered with a kiss that left her toes tingling.

"Oh, Jake. Wow." Her fingers wove deep into his hair, and she lifted her face, eager for more.

"What am I going to do with you, Angel?" His mouth lowered—

Suddenly, she jerked back. The wheel let out a horrific squeal, and she wanted to shriek along with it.

The wheel began to move. Angel straightened, her heart racing in her chest. She patted her hair with trembling fingers.

What am I going to do with you?

What had she been thinking? Kissing him like that? More importantly, what had *he* been thinking? He'd responded as if she were a woman rather than a child.

Disappointment rose from the depths of her soul. She knew she should be rejoicing that she'd succeeded in breaking down another barrier between them. That's what she'd been hired to do, wasn't it?

Why then did she feel so bad? And why couldn't she shake the feeling that this was all wrong?

They were almost at the bottom. In seconds, the attendant would open the metal bar that had held them in, and they'd be back in the real world... where he was her teacher...where she was his student...where she still had a case to break.

She forced a smile. "So when do you want to do this again?"

The phone only rang once before he answered. "Dan Reilly."

She smiled at the familiar raspy voice. "It's me. Angel."

"Sweetheart, it's past midnight." Worry edged his words. "Is anything wrong?"

"Everything is fine. I just hadn't talked to you in a while and—"

"Angel. You don't call in the middle of the night to say hello. What's going on?" The police sergeant was smart and shrewd, and she knew he'd never settle for less than the truth. He'd also never let up until she told him. "I was talking to a friend tonight…"

She hesitated, but the memory of Jake's regret spurred her forward. Angel took a deep breath. "Anyway, this guy happened to mention how his brother died and he'd never even told him he loved him and…"

"You thought of me."

"No." Her cheeks grew hot. "I mean, yes."

"Honey, I've known you a long time. I know how hard it is for you to say what you feel."

Of course, he knew. He'd been more of a father to her than anyone. But Jake's words had hit close to home and made her realize she'd never told the man that had rescued her from the streets all those years ago what he meant to her.

"I love you, Dan," Angel said simply. "You saved my life that day. Then you saved my soul when you brought me to Christ. I can never thank you enough."

"You've repaid me many times over, sweetheart." The man's voice was husky. "You've been like a daughter to me all these years. I've watched you grow into a fine Christian woman who lives her faith. I couldn't ask for more."

Tears welled up in Angel's eyes and she let them slip down her cheeks, not even bothering to brush them aside. "I'd better let you go. It's getting late. You take care."

"You, too," he said softly. "And, Angel..."

Her fingers tightened around the receiver. "Yes, Dan?"

"I love you, too."

Angel dropped the phone into its cradle and leaned her head back against the sofa. Her thanks was long overdue. Now she would have no regrets, whether Dan lived one more day or fifty years.

She smiled. God had brought Dan into her life when she'd needed him most. Now He'd brought Jake. Only God knew if he was destined to be just a brief player in her life or part of some greater plan.

Meeting Jake had already had an impact. Hadn't she finally said the words she should have said years ago to Dan? Why was it so hard to tell those who mattered most to you how you felt?

Angel lifted her eyes heavenward and thanked the One who'd been her strength these past ten years. From now on she wouldn't hesitate to say "thank you" or "I love you," frequently and loudly, to both God and her fellow man.

What about Jake? a tiny voice inside whispered. *Are you going to tell him "thank you"? What about "I love you"?*

She pushed the ridiculous thought aside. Dan was right. It was late. And she must be even more tired than she realized.

Chapter Nine

Jake searched his memory and visualized a tall redhead with a penchant for tight clothing. After thinking for a moment, he added her name to the page. He stared in amazement at the growing list, surprised at how many substitutes he'd been able to remember.

He chuckled. Tom had been right. His mind was a steel trap, at least for some things.

If only everything could come that easy. His smile changed to a frown and he stared at the sheet. Tony D'Fusco was at the top of the page. If only Jake could be sure he'd get to the guy before the police did.

He'd already planned what he'd ask. He'd be subtle, nonthreatening, his questions designed to probe Tony's tie with Angel without alerting the guy to the fact that Jake had absolutely no idea what that relationship entailed.

Deep down, he couldn't believe that Angel could be involved in anything illegal. Despite her sometimes outrageous appearance, there seemed to be a genuine goodness that surrounded her like a halo.

You're just like your brother—you always look for the best in people. His mother's words rose unbidden from his childhood memories. She'd meant the words as a compliment to both him and Jim. Nancy Weston lived her faith and encouraged her sons to do the same. She was an incurable optimist who'd never hated a person in her whole life. She'd even managed to forgive Jim's killers, Jake thought with more than a little bitterness. It was, after all, the Christian thing to do. God's word was clear. Jake should forgive them, too. But he couldn't.

It had been part of the reason he'd stayed away from worship services. He shouldn't hate those kids, but he did. They'd stabbed his brother and left him to die. And Jake couldn't forgive them no matter what his parents or his pastor said. They hadn't been there. They hadn't watched Jim die.

Only Amanda had understood.

Amanda.

She was his one regret. Even though just a few months ago he'd convinced himself she was the love of his life, something had held him back from making a formal declaration.

Jake laid his pencil down and wiped a hand across his brow. He'd made such a mess of everything. Was he about to make another mistake by trying to handle this Angel mystery on his own? Maybe he should tell Tom what he'd discovered and let the principal take it from there. If only he knew the right thing to do.

"Jake? Honey, is something wrong?"

"Mother." His head jerked up at the familiar voice. "I didn't hear you come in."

"It's no wonder." His mother pulled up a kitchen chair next to him and sat down. "You were so lost in thought, I think I could have screamed and you wouldn't have heard me."

"I don't know about that," Jake said with a smile. "You have a pretty good set of lungs. Remember when that rat of Jim's got loose in the house and you tripped over him in the laundry room?"

"How could I forget?" His mother chuckled. Her full lips widened into a smile deepening the laugh lines encircling her mouth. With her auburn hair brushing her cheeks, she looked more like a mischievous sprite than the mother of two grown sons. "That creature almost gave me a heart attack."

"Jim loved that rat." Jake's smile faded and the familiar sadness returned.

"What's wrong, honey?" She looked concerned.

"I'm just tired," he said. "I've been busy."

"Too busy to return my calls?"

Heat rose up his neck. He ducked his head, unwilling to meet her eye. "Sorry about that."

"Your father and I haven't seen you in weeks."

Jake took a deep breath and lifted his gaze, his guilt compounded by the additional hurt he knew he'd caused. "I really am sorry."

His mother paused for a moment. She tilted her head and eyed him speculatively. "Is it Amanda? Are you and she—"

"Are we what?" Jake scowled.

"I don't know." Her face colored. "Getting serious? Maybe thinking about marriage?"

Jake heaved an exasperated sigh even while he knew he should be used to this. His mother was a romantic, still blissfully happy with her husband of thirty years. Her dream was to see him married and working on a whole "passel" of grandchildren.

Right now, he wished he had never introduced Amanda to his mother. Although the two of them hadn't spent any extended periods of time together, his mother had liked Amanda and often asked about her. In some ways it had probably been a mistake to keep the contact to a minimum. Once his mother had discovered Amanda wasn't a Christian, the pressure to marry would have ceased. Jake supposed he could tell her, but for whatever reason he didn't.

"Amanda and I are on the outs," Jake said. "We're really not seeing much of each other anymore."

"Why is that?" His mother was clearly perplexed, and he couldn't blame her. Last time they'd talked, he and Amanda were still dating.

But that had been before he'd started thinking more about his faith. And that was before Angel Morelli had been dumped into his life.

As if she could read his mind, a twinkle replaced the confusion in his mother's eye. "You've met someone else."

"No." He shook his head and waved a dismissive hand. "Of course not."

"Of course not?" Her voice rose, and she straightened in her seat, a clear sign of a lecture coming on. "You're twenty-six years old. It's past time for you to settle down. Your father and I—"

"—were already married and had two children by the time you were twenty-six," he finished automatically. He'd heard it so many times that he found himself mimicking his mother's inflection.

His mother laughed, her natural effervescence bubbling forth. "Oh, sweetheart, forgive me. You know I mean well. It's just that your father and I are so happy, and I want that for you."

"I know," he said quietly.

"If you and Amanda aren't together, maybe you could give my friend Jackie's daughter a call? She's only twenty-one but—"

"Mother. No." His voice was firm and the tone final. If he didn't put the brakes on her now, he'd have five dates by the end of the week. His mother had missed her calling. Instead of a real estate agent, she should have been a professional matchmaker.

"But why not? If you're not seeing anyone, what would it hurt?"

"Actually, I am." The words slipped from his lips so easily, it was as if they'd been poised there from the beginning.

"I knew it." His mother leaned forward to rest her elbows on the table. "Who is she? Do I know her? How did you meet? Can you bring her to dinner on Sunday?"

Fired with machine-gun-like precision, the questions shot forth one after the other with no breath in between.

"We could all go to church together."

"No," he snapped.

Hurt shone in her blue eyes, and guilt once again assailed him.

He cursed his abruptness. After all, he'd only wanted to quiet her down, not trample her feelings. Still, he couldn't afford to give in on this one. No way could he allow his mother to meet Angel.

"Mother." Jake gentled his tone. "Every time I introduce you to someone I'm dating, I swear, you start planning the wedding that night."

"I do admit I sometimes get carried away." His mother's lips twitched. Was she remembering the woman before Amanda? Only after they'd quit dating had he discovered his mother had reserved the church for a June wedding—after only their second date!

He raised a brow. "Sometimes?"

"All right. It's my one weakness." Her laugh sounded more like a giggle. "But I have only your best interest at heart."

That part, at least, was true. She'd never given him any reason to doubt her love or her good intentions.

"I know you have," he said gently. "But you have to respect my wishes on this.

"I don't get to meet your girlfriend?"

Hadn't she heard one word he'd said? "She's

not my girlfriend. And—'' She opened her mouth to speak, but he silenced her with a look. ''—even if she were, I've decided from now on to play it safe. The only woman I'll introduce you to is the one *I've* chosen to marry.''

It sounded radical, but he had no choice. Not if he didn't want to end up one day at his own wedding rehearsal before he'd even popped the question.

Despite her obvious disappointment, his mother's eyes still sparkled. ''I'm intrigued. You've never mentioned marriage before.''

Jake groaned out loud. ''Mother…''

''We'll talk about this later.'' She patted his hand, a satisfied smile on her lips. ''Right now I need to get going. I only meant to stay a minute.''

She pushed a strand of hair off his face with the back of her hand, then brushed a quick kiss across his cheek. ''You might want to stop by the barbershop on your way home from work tomorrow. You wouldn't want your new 'friend' to think you looked like a sheepdog.''

Jake could only shake his head. He didn't dare comment. Everything he'd said so far to stop her only seemed to egg her on. At least she hadn't commented on his T-shirt and jeans. Knowing her, if he wasn't careful, he'd come home to find a whole new wardrobe from Woodland Hills's most exclusive men's shop in his closet. It was just the kind of thing she'd do.

Still, she meant well. He rose and walked her to the door, his arm looped loosely about her shoulders. "I'm going to church tomorrow. Save me a seat?"

A look of such intense pleasure lit her face that Jake had to glance away. Why hadn't he realized how much he'd hurt her when he'd turned his back on God?

"You've finally been able to forgive—"

The warm glow that had momentarily filled his body vanished in the icy blast of reality. "I have not," Jake said sharply.

He should have expected this. Of course she'd assume he'd forgiven *them*. He took a deep breath and forced his voice to a more rational-sounding level. "I can't. Not right now. But I also can't stay away from the church, from my faith, any longer. Maybe someday I'll be able to forgive them. I don't know."

How about never, a voice inside whispered. *That's when you'll forgive them.*

Unexpectedly, her arms wrapped around him, and although she stood six inches shorter and a good seventy pounds lighter, he knew she was the strong one. "Pray, Jake. Ask God to help you. You don't have to do this alone. Let Him help you let go of the anger and hate."

Jake shut his eyes tight. He knew she was right. But he'd been there. He couldn't forget the pain in Jim's eyes and the blood. His hands clenched into fists. *The senselessness of it.*

His mother hugged him extra hard before stepping back. "By the way, this girl…this friend of yours…what color is her hair?"

Still lost in his thoughts, Jake answered without thinking. "Dark brown, almost black."

"What's her name?"

Immediately he realized he'd entered the danger zone. Although her words seemed careless and offhand, her expression was calculating.

He pressed his lips together. She could torture him, torment him, but she wasn't going to trick him again. "You never give up, do you?"

Her smile dimmed, and for an instant a shadow of sadness crossed her face. "I love you too much to do that. I want you to be happy."

"I am happy," he said, giving her a kiss goodbye.

As he watched her drive away, the realization that he'd actually meant the words washed over him.

When he was with Angel he felt like his old self again. Thank God, he'd decided to stop at the carnival. He almost hadn't. He'd been in the area when he'd caught sight of the lights. When they were little, he and Jim had gone every year. As they'd grown older, they'd taken their dates. That hadn't been nearly as much fun as last night.

Running into Angel had been an unexpected surprise. What a coincidence that they'd both been there, alone.

Or was it?

He paused. Surely she hadn't planned it? What purpose could she have? Unless it was for the same reason she was pretending to be a student?

Naw, that couldn't be it. He hadn't decided to go himself until the last minute. Jake shoved his doubts aside. If he didn't watch it, he was going to turn into another Tom Jorgens, determined to read something into nothing.

Jake returned to the kitchen, grabbed another cup of coffee and sat down. He stared at the list in front of him. One of these teachers could be the link to breaking a multi-state drug ring.

His gaze was drawn to Tony D'Fusco's name. His jaw tightened. He'd liked Tony. Tony had been an excellent teacher and had seemed like an-all-around good guy.

Tomorrow, he'd double his efforts to reach Tony. He had to find him before the police did.

He had to know what his connection was to Angel.

* * *

Jake spent Monday morning at the school district's central administration office. It took the entire morning. By the time the meeting concluded, Jake wanted nothing more than to relax over lunch before heading back to his afternoon classes. But he had more pressing matters on his mind.

He headed down the long hallway, admiring the shiny linoleum and fresh paint that made the turn-of-the-century building look almost new. Jake stopped in the doorway of a large room. A maze of cubicles lay spread out before him. The tall mauve and gray panels effectively hid their inhabitants from view.

Debra Dean.

According to one of the administrators, her office was in this room. The irritation that he'd kept under control surged. There was no reason for her not to have returned his calls. All he wanted was an address or a phone number. Surely, that wasn't too much to ask?

A young girl, who didn't even look old enough to be out of high school, stopped, a friendly smile lighting her features. "Are you looking for someone?"

"Debra Dean."

The girl batted her eyes at him appreciatively. She was attractive, with her brown hair cut in wispy pieces and her short skirt showing off her shapely legs to full advantage, but she didn't look a day over eighteen.

"Debra sits over there." She smiled and pointed to a row of cubicles at the far edge of the room. "In that last aisle. She's about halfway back on your right."

"Thanks." He turned to go, but she stepped in front of him.

"If you need anything, my name's Callie." The girl pointed to a nearby cubicle. "I sit there. I do the payroll."

He smiled. "Jake Weston. Woodland Hills."

"I do the payroll for Woodland Hills." Her smile brightened.

"Is that right?" Jake feigned interest and stifled a groan at the glimmer of feminine interest in her eyes. "I'd better be going. See you around, Kellie."

"Callie," she corrected him.

He flashed her a smile. "Callie."

Debra's cubicle was just where the girl had said it would be, and Jake breathed a sigh of relief when he saw that the woman was actually at her desk.

He rapped lightly on the partition's metal edge. "Ms. Dean."

The woman removed the reading glasses and

pushed the computer reports she'd been reviewing to the side. "Yes?"

"I'm Jake Weston."

Confusion clouded her features, and Jake's heart sank. "We talked last week. You were going to help me get a current address and phone number of a friend...?"

"I remember now. You're the one from Woodland Hills." Debra started riffling through a stack of folders on the corner of her desk. "You know I used to teach with Tom Jorgens years ago. In fact, my husband and I used to socialize with Jane and Tom."

"You know Jane died a few years back."

"I know. I hear the guy that hit her is going to be back on the street." She sighed and set the folder down. "Every time I think of Jane, I can't help but remember her funeral. It was so hard for me. I know it's politically incorrect to talk religion, but in my mind there's nothing sadder than to go to a service where God isn't even mentioned... where eternal life isn't even brought up because the person left behind doesn't believe."

"I agree." Jake had been there and had thought the same thing. He couldn't help but remember Jim's funeral. There was no comparison between the two.

"How's Tom doing? Last time I saw him he looked terrible. He must have dropped a good thirty pounds. And unlike me—" Debra patted her own ample hips "—he didn't have any to lose."

Jake paused and steered a wide path around the weight issue. He'd learned long ago, it never paid to discuss that topic with any woman. But he didn't want to discuss Tom's grief, either. That would only feed the office's gossip mill. He chose his words carefully. "Tom's had a hard time of it since Jane died. I think he still really misses her."

"I imagine he does. I know I do." The woman sighed. "It was such a tragedy."

"Yes, it was. Ms. Dean, I wondered if you'd had a chance to look up—"

"Tony D'Fusco?" Debra Dean smiled and her fingers returned to the folders. "I pulled his file last week and I've been meaning to take a look at it and get back to you."

She opened a folder, stared at one page, flipped to another for a brief moment, then returned to the first. It was all Jake could do not to snatch it out of her hands.

"Find something?"

A frown furrowed her brow. "You didn't tell me your friend went to Italy."

"Italy?" Jake couldn't control his surprise. His voice rose.

"That's right."

His gaze followed her finger to where the tip of a red nail rested on the paper. "St. Stephen's?"

"It's a well-known liberal arts school in Rome. It looks like in his letter Mr. D'Fusco indicates he's going to be teaching English. Unfortunately, he didn't give us a phone number."

"That's all right," Jake said. "I can take it from here."

Debra wrote down the name of the school on a slip of paper and handed it to him. "Good luck. I hope you reach your friend."

Jake folded the paper and stuffed it into his pocket. "I guarantee you, I'll be talking to Tony before the end of the week."

Debra smiled. "Be sure and tell him we'd love to have him back."

"I sure will." Jake wished he didn't have to teach all afternoon. He couldn't wait to call Tony. Once Jake talked to him, he'd know if Angel was a cop or a part of some drug ring. If the man denied knowing her, it was probably the latter. Jake had already promised himself, if that happened he'd go straight to Tom with his suspicions. He'd have no choice.

"I said, is there anything else I can do for you, Mr. Weston?"

He flashed her a smile and shook his head. "No, Ms. Dean. I believe the rest is up to me."

Chapter Ten

"What do you mean he's following in the footsteps of Kings Stephen and Charles IV?" Jake gripped the receiver and counted to ten.

He'd made a special effort to time his call to St. Stephen's School so that he'd be able to speak directly with Tony. Now, it appeared he'd called a day too late.

The man on the other end rattled on, giving him more details about a spring trip to Budapest and Prague than he ever wanted to know. The only part that mattered was that they'd left yesterday, and that Tony had apparently gone with the students as a chaperone.

"When Mr. D'Fusco does get back, you'll make sure he gets my message?" Jake listened as the man repeated his name and phone number. "That's right. Could you please tell him that it's very important that I speak with him as soon as possible?"

Jake hung up the receiver and leaned back in the chair. The man had assured him that his message would be relayed at the earliest opportunity. But when that would be was anyone's guess.

For now, he'd just have to continue his watchful waiting.

Watching Angel every day.

And waiting to see if she'd give her true identity away.

Jake slunk low in the tattered seat of his parent's old Impala. His father only used the battered blue car for fishing trips and was more than agreeable to his son borrowing it for a "special project." In Angel's neighborhood, Jake's new Cherokee would have stuck out like a sore thumb. This car fit right in.

He'd been parked down the block from Angel's house for most of the afternoon. If he couldn't find out who she was from Tony, he'd have to try another avenue. Although he felt more than a little foolish, he'd decided to stake out her house and see what he could discover. Because most of the small homes didn't have driveways, cars lined both sides of the street, bumper to bumper. He'd been lucky to snag a prime spot, close enough for a clear view of her front door, but far enough back that she wouldn't notice him—he hoped.

He'd worried needlessly about the neighbors' reaction. No one even gave him a second glance. Apparently, in this area everyone minded their own business.

The streetlights at the far end of the block were just coming on when a small foreign car with a hanger for an antennae stopped in front of Angel's house. An older woman with bushy red hair that stuck out in all directions laid on the horn. A small child stood in the back seat staring out the window.

Angel's door swung open, and she bounded onto the porch, her dark hair pulled back beneath a ball cap.

"Hurry up, Angel." The redhead's voice was deep and booming and carried all the way down the block. "I'm running late."

Angel pulled the door shut with a *slam* and hurried down the steps.

Jake's fingers moved to the ignition, then stopped.

Angel had opened the passenger side door but hadn't slid inside the way he'd anticipated. Jake narrowed his gaze. She appeared to be pointing to the child.

To his surprise, the woman got out and buckled

the kid in the seat belt before taking her place back behind the wheel. The car backfired once and took off down the street in a cloud of blue smoke.

Jake followed at a safe distance, maneuvering his way through the evening traffic with ease. It wasn't long before the small car jerked to a stop in front of a run-down movie theater. Angel got out immediately, and had barely shut the door before the car took off.

Standing all alone on the sidewalk in the darkness, dressed only in a T-shirt, shorts and ball cap, Angel looked young and vulnerable. She shifted from one foot to the other, her gaze sweeping the surrounding area as if she were searching for something. Or someone.

To be safe, Jake waited until she went inside before he parked the Impala. Although there was a parking lot next to the theater, he chose a spot down the block on the street.

He bought his ticket from a pimply-faced girl, who seemed more interested in reading her book than in taking his money. She took so long, he expected Angel to see him standing there any minute and pepper him with questions he couldn't begin to answer.

He was thankful that by the time he finally got his ticket, the movie had already started and the lobby was deserted. He made it all the way inside without seeing Angel or anyone else he knew. The theater lights had dimmed, and Jake stood in the back shadows surveying his surroundings and letting his eyes adjust.

He spotted Angel immediately. She was about halfway down on the right. A big tub of popcorn sat in her lap and a super-size drink rested in her hand.

He couldn't help but smile. For someone so small, she sure had a mighty appetite. His stomach growled, reminding him how long it had been since he'd eaten, but he ignored it and looked for a good place to sit.

Toward the back of the theater on the left, an older man with thick bottle glasses chomped on a box of mints. In the same row an overweight woman a few seats away munched on her own tub of popcorn. Jake eased into their aisle and sat between them.

Slouching down, he fixed his gaze on Angel. And waited.

Awkward was the word, Angel decided. When Crow had called last night and asked her to a movie, she hadn't known what to say. Especially when she asked if he had business to discuss, and he said no.

And now he was late. Angel glanced at her

watch and took a sip of her large soda. She'd deliberately chosen a seat on the aisle. If Crow decided to show up, he shouldn't have any difficulty finding her.

The movie was half over before her partner appeared. He slid into the seat next to her, and even in the dim light she could see the tension in his face.

"What's up?" she whispered in his ear, grateful the nearest couple was five rows down.

"We need to talk." His voice was low and, for Crow, unusually kind. "But not here."

Her breath caught in her throat. Something was very wrong. "Tell me now."

He shook his head. "I'll take you home." Again a gentleness she'd never heard ran through his voice. "We'll talk there."

Their eyes met. A chill swept through her body. "It's something bad, isn't it?"

Abruptly Crow swore. Digging in the pocket of his jacket, he pulled out a vibrating pager and glanced at the number. His lips tightened. "I've got to go."

"But your news?"

A shadow crossed his dark eyes. "It'll have to wait."

"No. Tell me now."

He patted her awkwardly on the shoulder. "I can't. Not this way."

She grabbed his arm, more insistent this time. "Tell me."

He leaned his head back against the seat and exhaled deeply. "Dan Reilly was killed tonight."

Angel's body felt numb. "No."

He glanced down at his hands. "He was shot answering a domestic."

Dear God, no. Tears slipped in a steady stream down her cheeks, and Angel was barely conscious of Crow taking her in his arms, his breath warm against her hair.

"That's why I was late," he said. "I just heard."

"Why Dan?" She lifted her face and choked back a sob. "He was one of the good guys."

"I'm sorry, Angel. I know how close the two of you were."

Close? Close didn't begin to describe it. More tears slipped down her cheeks.

The pager in Crow's hand vibrated against her shoulder. She sat up straight and wiped the tears away with the back of her hand. "You need to go."

"I know I do." His gaze met hers. "Will you be okay?"

"I'll be fine." With great effort she forced her lips into a reassuring smile. "You be careful."

"I'll stop by later." Crow gave her shoulder a squeeze, and then suddenly she was alone.

Dan gone? Dead? How could that be? She'd talked to him less than a week ago.

She shut her eyes and prayed silently. *Dear God, you know how much Dan meant to me. I know he's with you, but I'm all alone now. Please help me.*

The pressure in her chest increased, and Angel bit her lip. She concentrated on breathing past the crushing pain. In and out. In and out. Until the sobs welling up from deep within her subsided. If she didn't think, she'd be fine. She could make it home. Then she could fall apart.

"Angel." A deep voice sounded beside her. For an instant she thought that Crow had returned. But this voice was lower and smoother.

She looked up into the concerned eyes of Jake Weston.

"Are you all right?" He squatted down next to her seat. "I saw Crow leave."

Confused, she could only stare. What was Jake doing here? She didn't want to see him now. She didn't want to talk to him. Her control hung tenuously on a rapidly fraying thread. One kind remark could snap it.

"I'm fine." Angel turned her face from his searching gaze. "I just want to be left alone."

"You've been crying." He brushed the wetness from her cheek with a finger. "What's wrong?"

"I'll tell you what's wrong." An irritated masculine voice answered from the middle section. "You two are talking, and I'm trying to watch the movie."

The thread started to snap. Angel pushed up from her seat, upsetting the popcorn that rested in her lap. Ignoring the mess, she swept the kernels from her jeans and grabbed her bag. "I've got to go."

Angel brushed past him and headed out the door. She blinked briefly in the bright lobby lights before the outside darkness enveloped her.

Angel stared at the half-empty parking lot until it hit her. Of course her car wasn't here. She'd caught a ride with a neighbor, assuming Crow could drop her off.

She was thankful the night was clear, although slightly chilly. Angel welcomed the cold, relishing the brisk air numbing her skin, wishing it could only freeze the pain burning deep inside.

Ignoring the fact that walking alone at night—especially in this neighborhood—was never advisable, Angel turned and headed down the sidewalk. She focused on putting one foot in front of the other. When thoughts of Dan surged, she started counting her steps. At five hundred sixty, the sound of a car motor caught her ear. At five hundred eighty, the vehicle slowed behind her.

Angel tensed, and her senses kicked into high alert. She looked ahead, then side to side. No help up ahead and nowhere to run.

She stopped by a tree and turned abruptly, her back protected by the trunk of a huge oak.

A blue Chevy she didn't recognize pulled up to the curb and shut off its lights. The interior was dark, and the nearest streetlight was half a block away.

The driver's side door opened. Angel's adrenaline pumped, and she readied herself. She could hold her own against one or two, but if there were more—

"I know you said you wanted to be alone..."

"Jake." She sagged against the tree. "You scared me to death. What are you doing here?"

Glad he'd taken that extra step and come after her, he smiled. "I thought you might want a ride."

He'd expected her to jump at the offer. To thank him for his kindness. He hadn't expected what he got.

Her eyes narrowed and her voice was positively frosty. "What part of 'I want to be alone' didn't you understand?"

"It's not safe to walk in this area." His jaw had a stubborn set to it.

"Thanks for the advice, *Dad*." Angel pulled her ball cap lower, hiding her eyes. "But I can take care of myself. I don't need you or anyone else telling me what to do."

If he didn't know better, he'd swear she *was* eighteen. She had the insolence typical of that age down to an art.

"C'mon, Angel. Get in the car." He reached out and grabbed her arm.

"Don't you touch me." She jerked back and stood before him with her fists knotted at her sides.

It was all Jake could do to hang onto his rising temper. She was being ridiculous, childish even. For goodness' sake, all he wanted to do was give her a ride home.

He stared at her face, pale in the moonlight, and some of his anger melted. Although the tears he'd seen earlier had vanished, the look in her eyes showed the pain was still with her.

"What did he say?" Jake asked softly. "To hurt you so much?"

Angel stiffened, and for a moment her bottom lip trembled. But then her expression grew stony. "Stay out of my business, Jake. None of this is any of your concern."

She whirled and stalked off down the sidewalk.

He wanted to call to her, to tell her it *was* his business. After all, weren't they friends?

In the end, he watched her go without saying another word. But as her friend and nothing more, he got back in his car and followed her from a distance all the way home.

Once she was safely inside, it made no sense to sit in a car that smelled like fish and watch her house. No sense at all. But for some reason Jake couldn't bring himself to leave.

About an hour after Angel returned home, Crow showed up. Jake wasn't sure how the guy even got there. He hadn't seen or heard a vehicle. But suddenly Crow was there, on the porch, under the light, lightly rapping with his bare knuckles on the wood screen door, his gaze constantly shifting as if any minute he expected someone to jump out of the darkness.

Crow knocked again, louder this time. The sound carried all the way to Jake's car.

She opened the door, an ethereal vision in a white T-shirt that hung to her knees.

Jake tensed and leaned forward, narrowing his gaze.

Crow raised a hand and brought it to her face.

Jake held his breath, waiting for her to tell the big guy where to get off, the way she had told Jake.

Perhaps she'd slam the door in his face. At the very least she should push his hand away.

But she fell into his arms. His lips lowered to her hair and his fingers splayed across her back, pulling her to him.

Jake looked away. He didn't know who she really was or what she was doing. All he knew was that he wished he didn't care.

Angel opened her eyes to sunlight streaming through her bedroom window. She scrunched her eyes shut, desperate to return to a dreamland where friends didn't die and happy endings were guaranteed. She reached out, yanked on the cord, and the venetian blinds dropped with a clatter. The light disappeared.

Satisfied, Angel padded across the floor, down the hall and into the bathroom. Swollen eyes and a blotchy face reflected back from the cracked bathroom mirror. She drew a shaky breath and wiped away fresh tears with the tips of her fingers. It was surprising there was any moisture left in her body. She thought last night would have drained her dry.

Thank goodness, Crow had been there for her. He'd been a true friend. For over two hours she'd talked and Crow had listened.

It had been a cathartic experience. Sharing stories about how she'd changed when God had brought Dan into her life gave her an untold measure of comfort.

Dan had died in the faith. She had no doubt of that. Though he was gone from this life, one day she'd see him again.

The only unfortunate part of the evening was when Crow blurted out that he thought he loved her. She'd been shocked. Why hadn't she seen this coming?

Because I only have eyes for Jake.

She'd tried to soften the blow, but Crow had been openly embarrassed when he realized she thought of him only as a friend. He'd left soon after, saying he should have known she'd prefer a pretty-boy like Weston.

So if she preferred Jake, why had she been so harsh with him? Even in her hurt and anger she'd known he was only trying to help. Why, then, did she push him away?

Obviously he didn't realize what he was asking. She sighed. *Trust him?* If only she could.

But not now. Not yet. Not until she knew for sure, without one shadow of a doubt, that her heart would be safe with him.

Chapter Eleven

If one more person entered Big Al's Burger Palace, Angel feared the establishment would burst at its seams. All the booths, tables and counter stools were full. A line that had started at the cash register now trailed all the way to the door.

Angel expelled an irritated sigh and resisted the urge to look at her watch again. Of all the times for Mike to be late. She'd held the booth for twenty minutes already, and if she didn't order soon she'd be tossed out the door. The Burger Palace was like that; greasy food fast, but not a lot of patience. Down time in a server's section meant fewer tips, and money was the bottom line.

The waitress had refilled her water glass three

times, the last time casting a pointed glance at the people waiting to be seated.

Angel decided to give Mike five more minutes. This would be her first drug buy from the boy, and she couldn't afford to miss this chance. If he hadn't shown by then, she'd have to consider her options.

"Hey, Mike. Over here," a voice across the room yelled.

"I'll catch you another time, man."

Angel looked up.

"Sorry." Mike slid into the seat opposite her. "Coach Deeter kept us late."

"What happened to Coach Weston?" Angel lowered her gaze and pretended to study the menu she'd already memorized.

Mike shrugged. "Someone said he'd gotten tied up in a meeting."

Angel's mind raced. From what she knew of Jake Weston, he rarely missed practice. What kind of meeting could have detained him?

"That Deeter, I can't believe the guy. He said we weren't taking practice serious enough." Mike snorted. "As if we're going to have any problem with TJ this weekend. They stink."

Thomas Jefferson High School was a rival, and even Angel, who didn't follow baseball, knew TJ sat at the bottom of the league standings. She smiled at Mike's cockiness. Never had he sounded more like a high school senior and less like a drug dealer.

"Did Ja—" she caught herself just in time "—Coach Weston ever show up?"

The boy's eyes turned sharp and assessing, and she knew he'd caught her gaffe. She braced herself for his questions, but they never came.

Instead Mike tossed his menu to the table, and, as if on cue, the waitress appeared. Only this time her manner was much more accommodating and all sense of urgency had vanished.

Angel stared. She could have sworn the girl's hair had been pinned back when she'd filled the water. Now the dark strands hung in loose curls around the elfin face and the lipstick looked to have been freshly applied.

The girl was in her chemistry class, and although she was one of those who'd never given Angel the time of day, from the undisguised interest that shone in her dark brown eyes, she appeared ready to give Mike the whole clock.

"Hi, Mike. Haven't seen you in a while."

"Caren." Mike shot the girl a dazzling smile, and Angel could immediately see why he had such a reputation with the girls. "Bring us two cheeseburgers and fries. I'll have a large chocolate malt and—"

Angel shook her head. "Water is all I want."

Caren slowly printed their order on a pad, all the while casting repeated adoring glances at Mike from beneath her lowered lashes. The task that should have taken only seconds stretched into minutes. Angel was thankful she and Mike had ordered the same thing or the girl would have been with them all night. Just when Angel was ready to suggest Caren pull up a chair, the girl flashed Mike a regretful backward glance and headed to a nearby table that for five minutes had been loudly demanding their bill.

Angel waited until she was sure the girl was out of earshot to speak. "Did you bring the stuff?"

Mike smiled. He reached over and grabbed her hand. "My dad says you shouldn't discuss business at the table."

She answered his smile with a sweet-as-pie one of her own and pulled her hand from his. "Yeah, and mine said to never mix business with pleasure."

The full-throated laugh that burst from the boy's lips took Angel by surprise. Those at nearby tables turned to look, but Mike didn't seem to care. Obviously he was used to being the center of attention. She decided to join in the fun and tossed in a girlish giggle of her own for effect.

By the time they'd stopped laughing, the waitress had returned with his malt balanced on a round tray. She handed him the tall glass, her fingers lingering a moment longer than necessary, her gaze plainly adoring. Unfortunately for her, Mike didn't even glance up. Instead he murmured an under-the-breath "Thanks," and kept his gaze fixed firmly on Angel.

Despite the fact that the girl had been downright rude to her in Chemistry, Angel almost felt sorry for her. The key word being *almost*. She couldn't resist giving the snobbish Caren a smug smile. After all, playing an immature teenager should have some advantages.

Oblivious to the girlish antics, Mike raised the glass to his lips and took a big swallow. "Man, that's good." He glanced at Angel's water. "Sure you don't want any?"

"Positive."

He gave Caren a dismissive glance. "That'll be all for now."

The girl turned in a huff, and Angel hid a smile. This was turning out to be a drug buy unlike any other.

When she'd first contacted Mike about buying some stuff for a "friend," he'd stalled, saying he'd have to get back to her. Then, when they'd finalized the arrangements, instead of meeting at a quiet out-of-the-way location, he'd not only picked the ultra-popular Burger Palace but had insisted they meet right after practice, a time when the place was always packed.

Now, he'd surprised her again. There was no sense of urgency, no rushing through the deal. He sat sipping his malt, acting as if he didn't have a care in the world—or a gram of crystal meth—in his pocket.

She wondered if Crow could be right. When she'd expressed her puzzlement over the meeting time and place, her partner hadn't thought it strange at all. He'd seen it before. For some, he said, the risk was the real high.

Since the guy seemed in no hurry to get down to business, Angel filled the silence with a topic near to the boy's heart. "Sounds like the baseball team will be going to state."

"Give it up, Angel. You're so transparent." His smile softened the harshness of his words. "You don't care about baseball. The reason you're interested in the team doesn't have a thing to do with the game."

"Really?" Angel rested her head on her hand and widened her eyes, pretending to hang on his every word. "Tell me more, oh wise one."

"It's not the game that turns you on." Mike leaned back and took another sip of his malt. "It's Coach Weston."

For a second Angel's breath caught in her throat.

Then she quickly recovered and rolled her eyes. "Yeah, right," she scoffed. "The guy's practically ancient."

Mike shrugged. "Deny it all you want. I've seen the way you look at him."

Angel groaned to herself. Surely, she hadn't been that obvious. She chuckled. "What can I say? He's hot. A girl can't help but notice."

The boy raised one eyebrow and shot her a wicked grin. "Or touch?"

His gaze riveted to hers. She swallowed hard, raised her chin. "I admit I'm hot and bothered, but it's not over something Jake Weston has." She lowered her voice to a sultry whisper. "Honey, you've got what I want."

The look of surprise that flashed across the boy's face was quickly replaced by one of pure masculine interest. She gave herself a mental pat on the back. This was too easy.

Mike leaned closer, and the chocolate scent of the malt mingled with his designer cologne. "I'll give you whatever you want, baby."

She smiled at his arrogance. "Are you sure?"

"Your wish is my command."

Their heads were now so close that her hair brushed his cheek. She spoke slowly and her lips barely moved. "Give me my crystal."

He jerked back and stared dumbfounded. "Is that all you want?"

"You're my best friend's guy." Angel kept her voice light. "I'm afraid even if I wanted to—" she traced a line down his cheek with her finger "—touch, I couldn't. You're off-limits."

Though he couldn't quite hide his disappointment, he seemed to understand. And Angel had achieved her purpose—she'd gotten the topic off Jake Weston.

The waitress brought their food, and though Angel had had a big lunch, she dove into her cheeseburger as if she hadn't eaten in a week. At least when your mouth was stuffed with food you couldn't talk. She'd grown tired of the banter and tired of the games. And mostly, tired of the wait.

The last bite of the greasy burger had barely cleared her lips when she made a big show of glancing at her watch. "Look at the time." She wadded up her paper napkin and tossed it on her plate. "I need to get going."

"You brought the money?" he asked quickly, his voice all business.

She was now thankful that he now seemed ready to get this show on the road, too.

"I'll walk you out." He laid a twenty on the table and followed her through the cluttered throng, greeting most of their fellow students by name, some with slaps on their backs.

Angel could sense their curious stares, and she made a mental note to give Emily the scoop before some well-meaning "friend" did. Not that she thought Emily would care at this point. Kenneth had started calling, and the girl was ecstatic. It appeared Ken was now "in" and Mike was on his way "out."

Crisp and unusually cool, the outside air was a refreshing change from the stifling warmth of the crowded Big Al's. Angel stopped on the sidewalk and waited for Mike to make his move. What was his plan? Surely even a risk-taker wouldn't do the exchange in broad daylight in full view of passersby.

Mike cupped her elbow in his hand and pointed to a jet-black sports car across the parking lot. "C'mon."

They walked past the busy drive in an area where carhops in short pink dresses brought the orders out to those who preferred to eat in their vehicles. The girls were cute and adorable in their 1950s-style outfits. Mike didn't give them a second glance.

He disarmed the car alarm and unlocked the doors with the remote. Angel climbed into the passenger seat and waited while he went around the front. He slid in on the driver's side, but instead of starting the engine as she expected, he sat there.

"I brought the money." She slipped her hand into her pocket and pulled out the bills.

It was almost as if she'd offered him a tissue, a napkin or something else of little value. Without a word or a second glance, Mike took the money and dropped the bills into a compartment filled with CDs.

"Aren't you going to count it?"

A little smile played at the corners of his lips. His arms slipped companionably around her shoulders, and he pulled her close, tucking a postage-stamp-size packet into her front shirt pocket in the process. "Why should I count it? You know better than to cheat me."

She gazed into his boyishly handsome face. The laughing eyes were now dead serious. Suddenly he looked too much like the kids of her youth, the ones on a fast track to nowhere. A wave of sadness swept over her. Mike had too much going for him to be wasting time heading down the wrong path.

She reminded herself that the sooner he was caught, the sooner he could turn his life around. She smiled up at him and pushed lightly against his chest, putting some distance between them. "The money's not the problem, Mike, my man.

The problem is, you've only given me enough for one little party and that'll be gone after tonight.''

His gaze sharpened. ''How much do you want?''

''An eight-ball should do it.'' She flashed him a bright smile. ''At least, for starters.''

Yes, the sooner she could bust this case, the better for them all.

Chapter Twelve

"I wouldn't go in there if I were you." Tom Jorgen's secretary leaned across her desk and spoke in a hushed tone. "He's in one of his moods."

At sixty-four and holding, Wilma McKenzie was known as the sea of calm in the turbulent waters of the high school office. Serene and unflappable, she rarely frowned, and laughter usually twinkled in her blue eyes partially hidden behind bifocals. She looked, Jake thought, like a kindly grandmother.

"That bad?" Jake paused. Wilma had been Tom's personal secretary for the past five years and had borne the brunt of his erratic mood swings since Jane had passed away.

"This is one of the worst." She shook her head. "He seemed okay this morning, but now—watch out."

"Any idea what set him off?" Jake kept his tone even and his facial expression deceptively composed. Could Tom have discovered that Angel wasn't eighteen and that Jake had known about it? Was that what was behind this last-minute summons that had left Jake scrambling? Surely, it had to be important for Tom to pull him out of baseball practice with State Tournaments coming up.

The secretary took off her glasses and rubbed the bridge of her nose with trembling fingers. Jake frowned. This was more serious than he'd thought.

"I'm not sure." She blinked several times rapidly. "The only thing I can tie it to is the mail."

Jake raised a brow. "Really?"

"When I brought it in, he was fine. Of course, he looked terrible. I don't think he's been sleeping well. But when I came back a few minutes later with some files he'd asked for, he practically bit my head off."

The older woman's lips quivered, and even though she ducked her head to pretend to be looking in the desk drawer, he caught a glint of tears in her eyes.

Jake's lips tightened. Tom had no right to take his anger out on Wilma. No right at all.

"Are you okay? Is there anything I can do?" Jake laid his hand on the woman's shoulder.

The secretary drew a ragged breath and straightened in her seat. Within seconds the implacable Wilma McKenzie was back, her face serene and her eyes so clear and dry that Jake wondered if he'd imagined the tears.

"I can handle anything that man can dish out."

Who was she trying to convince? Jake or herself?

"The point is, you shouldn't have to," Jake said softly. It was almost as if Tom had attacked his own mother. "I'm going to have a talk with him."

"Don't," Wilma said quickly. "Please. You'll only make it worse."

"He can't treat you like this."

"Let it go." The door to Tom's office jerked open, and Wilma mouthed *"Please."*

"About time you got here." The principal was clearly agitated, and little beads of sweat dotted his forehead. Rumpled and wrinkled, his normally impeccable suit looked as if he'd slept in it. Dark circles underscored his eyes, emphasizing the thinness of his face and sallow complexion. "I don't have all day."

Jake opened his mouth to tell the man he was right on time, but Wilma shot him a warning glance, and he closed it without speaking. Tom was like a wounded grizzly, clearly irritated and ready to attack.

Tom shut the door firmly behind Jake and gestured to a chair near the desk. Jake sat down and pretended not to notice that Tom's hand shook as badly as that of an alcoholic in the throes of withdrawal.

Instead of sitting, Tom paced the office. "I haven't slept in three days."

Jake's brow furrowed, his anger replaced by concern. "What's the matter? Are you sick?"

"Sick?" Tom gave a little laugh. "I'm sick all right, but not in the way you mean."

The principal stopped in front of his window and rested his hands on the sill, his back to Jake. "I don't know if you've read about it in the papers. But that slime-bag that killed my Jane is up for parole."

"But it's been barely two years." No wonder Tom was upset. The drunk driver that had smashed Jane's import into an unrecognizable mass of twisted steel had been convicted of motor vehicle homicide. The ten-year sentence the guy had received had given them all some degree of comfort.

"Apparently they're counting the time he served prior to the sentencing as well as giving him credit for good behavior." Tom's fist slammed into the wood sill, and he whirled around, pain etched on every line of his face. "It's not fair, Jake. He killed her as sure as if he'd shot her with a gun! And now, two years and he's free?"

"They won't let him out." Jake spoke with more confidence than he felt. His faith in the legal system had been rocked by the light sentences his brother's killers had received. Of course, they'd been tried as minors. The guy that had killed Jane had been an adult. "Not this soon."

"That's what I thought. Until I started hearing how people were writing to the parole board in support of his release." An expression of disgust crossed Tom's face.

"You can't be serious."

"I am serious." The principal's voice rose, and his eyes took on a wild appearance. "They're going to let the guy walk. And that's not all. Can you believe he had the nerve to ask for my forgiveness? He killed my wife and he thinks I'll forgive him?"

Forgiveness.

A band tightened around Jake's chest, constricting his breathing and making talking difficult. "You spoke with him?"

"If I ever got that close to him, he wouldn't need to worry about parole." Tom's voice, though quiet, had an ominous quality. Hatred solidified his face into a stony mask. "He'd be dead."

Even though Jake had often wondered what he'd

do if he ever came face to face with Jim's killers, he'd never considered murder. He exhaled a long breath. "You don't mean that."

"Don't I? What do you think I should do? Shake his hand and say, 'You killed my wife, of course I forgive you.'" He threw a wadded up piece of paper on the desk next to Jake.

Jake stared at the crinkly ball but made no move to pick it up. Before this moment, he hadn't realized just how much Tom had changed. Lately, there were few reminders of the good-natured, almost jovial, principal who'd hired Jake five years earlier, the man who'd quickly become his friend and his mentor. That man would never have reduced his secretary to tears or wanted to kill another human being. Was this what hatred did?

"Look at it." Tom shoved the paper into Jake's hand. "I can't believe he'd even ask."

Carlos and Anton have found the Lord. They're asking for your forgiveness. His response to his mother had been much the same as Tom's. He'd stared, angry she'd even ask. Angry that her ridiculous request still had the power to stir up all those feelings he'd worked so hard to bury. Angry that he felt guilty over saying what was in his heart: "I can't believe they'd think I'd forgive them."

"It's amazing, isn't it?" Jake said now, shaking

his head in disgust. "They think all they have to do is say they're sorry."

"I knew you'd understand." Tom sighed and collapsed into his desk chair.

Jake picked up the paper and tried to give it back, but Tom waved it away. "Read it. It's good for a laugh."

Reluctantly, Jake unwrapped the ball, flattening it smooth with the palm of his hand. The writing was clear, written in easily readable print.

"Read it aloud."

Jake shook his head. "I don't—"

"Read it," Tom said sharply. The wild look once again filled the man's eyes.

If Jake was going to calm his friend down, it appeared he had no choice but to do as Tom asked.

Jake cleared his throat.

Dear Mr. Jorgens,
This letter is long overdue. I haven't written before because I didn't know what to say.

Tom snorted and Jake paused, but Tom impatiently motioned for him to continue.

I still don't know what to say except I'm sorry. If I could exchange places with your wife I'd do it. I had no business getting behind that wheel and trying to drive home. With that one reckless action I deprived your wife of her life and you of her companionship and love. I also deprived my own wife and daughter of a husband and father for these past two years.

I deeply regret my actions that night and will carry the guilt with me until the day I die. I hope that one day you will find it in your heart to forgive me.

Sincerely,
John Andrews

The simple words rang true and unexpectedly touched a chord in Jake's heart.

"Can you believe it?" Tom raked his sweat-dampened hair back with his hand. "Sincerely, my—"

"Tom." Jake raised his gaze from the letter. "Maybe the guy really is sorry."

Visibly stunned at Jake's response, Tom could only stare.

Jake decided to take advantage of the opportunity. He chose his words quickly but carefully. "You notice he didn't make any excuses. He's had two years to think about what he's done. Everyone makes mistakes."

"Mistakes!" Tom bellowed so loudly that Jake

was surprised the windows didn't shatter. "The man kills my wife, and you call it a *mistake?!*"

Jake held out his hand. "Tom, that's not what I mean and you know it."

"I thought you of all people would understand." Tom stood and gripped the edge of the desk. He leaned forward across the surface until he was right in Jake's face. "So, tell me, Jake. Have you forgiven those two little hoodlums who killed your brother for their 'mistake'? How are you going to feel when they're back running the streets?"

The invisible band around his chest tightened another notch. "Drop it, Tom."

"What's the matter?" A snarl curved Tom's lip. "Am I hitting too close to home?"

Shoving his chair back with a clatter, Jake stood. He didn't have to listen to an obviously irrational man rant and rave. The fact that Tom's ramblings made some sense was shoved aside. "We'll talk later. I need to get going."

When he reached the doorway, Jake couldn't resist one last backward glance. Tom's mouth was spread in a thin-lipped smile. His arms were folded across his chest and a knowing expression blanketed his face. This time his voice was calm. "You can't forgive your brother's killers any more than I can forgive this drunk."

Jake jerked the door open.

"Don't get all high and mighty on me, Jake Weston. We're two of a kind, you and I."

Two of a kind.

Jake slammed the door shut.

Tom's words followed him through the thick wood and echoed in his head all the way down the hall. Tom's hate-twisted face and empty eyes filled his field of vision.

Once outside, Jake headed for the parking lot. There was no reason to stop at the ball field. His meeting with Tom had taken so long that practice would be long over. He jumped into his Jeep, intending to go straight home. Minutes later, Jake found himself sitting at Big Al's Burger Palace drive-in, ordering a hamburger and a soda.

How had he ended up here? It was as if the vehicle had had a will of its own. Jake blew out a breath and wondered if there was time to cancel his order. He wasn't even hungry.

His gaze searched the parking lot for the pony-tailed blond carhop. It stopped abruptly on a familiar low-slung sports car parked in the lot. He recognized Mike Blaine immediately. It took him a few more seconds to recognize Angel Morelli.

Jake tried to quell the anger that was building in him. What was Angel doing with Blaine? What kind of game was she playing now?

The boy was young enough to be her son. Well,

maybe not her son, but there was a big difference between an eighteen-year-old kid and a twenty-six-year-old woman. The wave of jealousy that hit Jake nearly took his breath away. Of course, Mike could just be giving her a ride home. Jake knew he should look away, give them their privacy.

But he kept his gaze fixed, even while tossing a few bills on a tray and grabbing his burger and soda from the blonde who'd finally showed up.

The two heads drew closer. Jake narrowed his eyes.

Mike slipped his arm around Angel's shoulder. A bite of hamburger stuck in Jake's throat.

Angel's hand rose and pushed against Mike's chest. Jake's hand moved to the door latch.

Suddenly the door on the passenger side of Mike's car opened. Angel hopped out, her dark hair gleaming in the sunshine.

He swallowed and leaned back against the seat, suddenly exhausted. Out of the corner of his eye he saw the sports car round the corner and disappear in traffic.

"Can I get you anything else, sir?"

He bolted upright at the cocky voice. A slice of pickle felt as if it dropped straight to his lungs.

Jake turned and looking into laughing brown eyes. "Angel!"

* * *

Without waiting for an invitation, Angel pranced around the front of the Jeep, opened the door and hopped into the passenger seat. "Give me a ride home?"

With her saucy smile and devil-may-care attitude, the girl looked like an impudent sprite against the cream-colored leather interior. Her dark hair was pulled back from her face in clips and hung in loose curls to her shoulders. Her white cotton shirt was dotted with tiny spring flowers and her short denim skirt barely reached mid-thigh. Today, even Jake found it hard to believe she was a day over eighteen.

"Now, why would I want to do that?" He raised a brow.

"Because." She smiled. "You're a good guy."

"Yeah, right," he said with a wry grin. "If I was a good guy, I wouldn't be hanging out here with you."

He'd meant the words to be a condemnation of himself—a teacher consorting with a supposed student—but the look that skittered across her face told him she had taken it far differently than he'd intended.

"I'm sorry. I didn't mean—"

"I think I'll catch a ride with Jarvis." She reached for the door latch.

"No." Jake practically shouted the word. Thoughts of her in the same vehicle with Big J sent a chill down his spine. He'd overheard Jarvis bragging in the locker room about his conquests one too many times. "I don't want you in a car alone with that guy. Understand?"

Angel paused and slowly turned back toward him. Her hand lingered on the door handle, but she no longer seemed in a hurry to leave.

Jake knew if Amanda had been in Angel's place, she'd have immediately puffed up and told him in no uncertain terms that she'd ride with whom she wanted, when she wanted. But Angel was not as impulsive as Amanda, not so prone to speak first and have regrets later.

She studied him for a moment until her tense expression eased. Then her lips lifted in a slight smile, and Jake sighed in relief.

"I was only looking out for you."

"I realize that." In spite of her youthful appearance, there was maturity in Angel's gaze. "I didn't want to go with him, anyway." Her nose wrinkled. "I don't like Beemers."

Jarvis's new BMW convertible had been the talk of the school last month. With its mirror ebony finish and its sporty styling, there had been no shortage of Woodland Hills students wanting to take a spin—most of them female.

"Lots of girls think Jarvis is *the* man."

Jake groaned to himself. He spent every day with teenagers. Now he was starting to sound like one!

"In case you hadn't noticed," Angel said lightly. "I'm not like the other girls."

"That's right." Jake let his gaze drop, focusing for a moment on her lips. "You're more mature."

Jake couldn't help but remember how sweet those lips had been. How close he'd felt to her that night on the Ferris wheel. His eyes explored her face; the gleam reflected in her eyes told him she remembered, too.

The brisk north breeze had turned the outside air unseasonably cold, but in the Jeep the temperature shot upward. Jake's breath grew ragged.

"We had a good time together the other night." Her dark eyes glittered. "Why haven't you called me?"

Jake stalled. She wasn't really a high school senior, but seeing her every day in his classroom made it hard to remember that fact. "I'm your teacher. Teachers don't call students for dates, no matter how *mature* they are."

For an instant, a flash of something that looked like approval crossed her face. But when she snorted and heaved a theatrical sigh, Jake was sure he'd been mistaken.

"Oh, brother," she said. "A man of conscience."

Jake laughed. She made integrity sound like a dirty word. "It's hard, but somebody's got to take a stand."

"Enough already. I just ate." Angel rolled her eyes. "Just tell me this isn't your way of getting out of giving me a ride."

"Angel." He pinned her with his gaze and spoke the words slowly and distinctly. "I want to give you a ride."

"You do?"

He nodded. God forgive him, he did. There were a thousand reasons he should keep his distance. She'd lied to him. He couldn't trust her. None of it mattered. He couldn't help wanting to be with her. "I've missed you."

"I've missed you, too," she said simply. Her face reddened the instant the words left her lips, as if she, too, had revealed more than she'd intended.

"Jake—"

Her husky voice sent a shiver racing down his spine.

She lightly rested her hand on his forearm. "One more thing?"

A horn blared, and Angel shot a quick glance out the window. Jake kept his gaze fixed on Angel and ignored the irritating sound.

He moved his arm so her hand slid down to his, and he gently locked their fingers together. "What is it you want, Angel? Tell me."

"Can I have a sip of your soda?" Her lips tilted upward in the barest hint of a smile. "I'm really thirsty."

Chapter Thirteen

Angel drained the last of Jake's cola with a noisy slurp. He didn't look her way.

They hadn't spoken since they'd left Big Al's. She didn't blame him for being annoyed. She'd teased him since she'd gotten in his car, and when he'd finally responded she'd shut him down.

He'd been ready to kiss her, and she'd been ready to let him—when that blasted horn had blared and she'd caught a glimpse of Marylou from her history class sitting in the next car, blatantly staring. What could Angel do but improvise? Unfortunately, the best she'd been able to come up with had been that ridiculous request for a drink.

She had to protect Jake's reputation. Big Al's was a well-known hangout for Woodland Hills staff and students. If he'd kissed her in full sight of everyone, his career would have been over. For a man of conscience, his behavior made no sense.

But then, why was he at the drive-in in the first place? He certainly hadn't stopped there because he was starving and couldn't wait until he got home to eat. Hungry men didn't leave a good half of Big Al's famous Mega Burger on their plate.

She wished she could forget the fleeting thought that had crossed her mind when she'd first spotted his Jeep. Even if Jake were involved in the drug ring, what purpose would there be in watching Mike do a sale? More than likely, his showing up had been purely coincidental. In fact, if she were a gambler she'd bet all her chips that Jake was what he appeared to be—a genuinely good person.

But she wasn't a gambler, she was a cop. She could leave nothing to chance.

"How was your meeting?"

"Meeting?" His expression was clearly puzzled.

"The reason you missed practice?"

"Oh, that." Worry lines appeared between his brows. "Mr. Jorgens had some things that he needed to discuss with me."

"Like?"

"Like none of your business." He softened his words with a smile.

Actually, Angel wasn't the least bit offended by

his brusqueness. Of course it was none of her business, but this was an investigation. She had to ask.

She shrugged and punched some buttons on his radio until she found her favorite station. An Elvis classic blared from the Jeep's speakers, and Angel joined in on the refrain. She made up the words she didn't know. When the song ended, she turned to find Jake staring.

She smiled and pushed back a strand of hair. "Do I have dirt on my face?"

He shook his head.

"What then?" Angel reined in her smile at a horrific thought. "I've got food in my teeth, and you don't want to tell me."

Quickly she pulled down the visor and flipped open the vanity mirror. Grinning broadly like an ape in a zoo, she scanned her teeth. Finding nothing, she closed the mirror with a *snap*. She heaved an exaggerated sigh. "Don't scare me like that again."

"You said once you grew up in East St. Louis." Jake said. "You moved from there…?"

"When I was fifteen," she answered automatically, shifting her gaze out the window. She rarely thought of those days anymore. Look Ahead was her motto.

"You always seem so happy," Jake said. "Yet that couldn't have been an easy life."

"It wasn't easy. You're right about that." She took a deep breath, determined to be as honest as she could without blowing her cover. "My parents died when I was ten. I was in and out of foster homes until I was fourteen. Then my aunt and uncle took me in…"

Her voice trailed off. Even after all these years it was still hard to think of that time without pain.

"It must have been a relief, finally being with family." He shot her a hopeful smile, and she knew that this was a guy who wanted to believe in happy endings.

"You'd think so, wouldn't you?" Angel sighed. "Unfortunately it didn't take me long to discover that my aunt couldn't have cared less if I was in the house or not, and that my uncle wanted the money from Social Services, not me. At least at the foster homes, I went in knowing the score."

"Like the one you're in now."

"What?"

"The foster home on Dempster. Is it better than being with your aunt and uncle?"

"Living on the street would beat living with them." Angel gave a wry smile. Her mind drifted back, remembering that dump of an apartment. The filth. The roaches. The people coming and going at all hours of the day and night. Her aunt drank continuously and her uncle worked sporadically.

Their survival depended on giving their constant visitors what they wanted.

"It sounds as if they had some problems."

"That's the understatement of the year." She chuckled, a dry humorless sound even to her own ears. There was nothing amusing about her time with them. After all, what was funny about an uncle taking a fifteen-year-old with him on a drug buy to allay suspicion? Or shoving his own niece in front of him when the buy started to go south? What could you say about a guy so low that he'd let his sister's child take a bullet meant for him?

"There was a time when I could have lit a match and watched them both burn."

If he was surprised at the vehemence in her tone it didn't show. Instead he seemed puzzled. His brows drew together in a frown. "But now?"

"I wasted a lot of time being angry. Angry at my parents for dying and leaving me alone. Angry at my aunt and uncle." She stopped and took a deep steadying breath.

She'd forgiven the man, she truly had. But his betrayal and her aunt's unwavering support of his actions still hurt. Angel blinked back the unexpected tears.

Jake's hand closed around hers. "You don't have to say any more."

"I know," she said softly. "But I haven't gotten to the best part."

"I'm glad it got better."

"Only because I changed." The hate and anger she'd harbored in her heart had nearly destroyed her. It would have, too, if not for Dan. "I committed my life to the Lord when I was sixteen. A friend helped me to see that if God could forgive everything I'd done, could I do any less for Aunt and Uncle?"

"You make it sound simple." A muscle in Jake's jaw jumped. "It's not that easy."

"Of course, it's not easy." Angel thought of the hours she'd spent in prayer. "You don't go from wishing someone dead to being their best friend. My uncle and I will never be close. But I no longer hate him. Instead I feel sorry for him and for the lifestyle he continues to lead."

"How did you ever do it?"

"I prayed," she said simply. "And when I thought there was no way I could forgive, I remembered grace is something *needed* but not *deserved*. I didn't deserve to be forgiven for my sins, but God forgave me. My uncle certainly didn't deserve to be forgiven—but how could I do any less for him than God had done for me?"

Angel waited for a response, a simple acknowledgment that he'd understood the point.

When he remained silent, she longed to fill the void, to talk more about her faith and the difference one person can make. But she'd learned long ago that you couldn't push someone into acceptance.

The silence continued until he pulled up to the curb in front of her house. "I'm sorry, Angel. You deserved so much better."

"It was bad," she acknowledged. "But I've met many who had it worse."

"Still…"

"No, really." She lifted her hand. If there was one thing she didn't need or want it was his pity. "When I found Christ, I gained a best friend. A friend that I can count on, that I can lean on. One that will never disappoint me, the One that makes all things possible."

His gaze sharpened. "Even forgiving the unforgivable?"

"Nothing is unforgivable." Angel could sense his pain, and her heart went out to him. She remembered her own struggles with the concept of grace. "With God's help anything is possible. That includes forgiving someone you never thought you could."

"You really believe that?"

She nodded. "I do."

Now free from the prying eyes of the Burger

Palace patrons, Angel slid across the seat until her shoulder touched his.

She knew what it was like to feel all alone, to struggle. If only she could give Jake half as much as Officer Dan had given to her—the comforting words from the Bible, the caring touch of another human being.

Angel wrapped her arm around Jake's and rested her head against his shoulder. "I'll pray for you, Jake."

The motor continued to idle. They sat for the longest time without speaking—two people who'd seen firsthand the worst life had to offer and who'd survived. But Jake needed to take the next step, Angel realized. He had to forgive if he was to move on. If only he would realize he wasn't in this alone.

Please, God. Let him feel Your strength.

Angel brushed a quick kiss across his cheek, opened the door and slid out.

By the time she'd walked halfway up the walk, a sense of uncertainty filled her. Maybe she should have talked more about God's grace and mercy? Or perhaps focused more on the power of prayer?

Dear God, I tried my best. I really did.

"Angel." His voice stopped her in her tracks. "You're not a high school senior."

Her breath caught in her throat, and she turned to face him. "I'm not?"

"No." Jake shook his head and shifted the Jeep into reverse. He spoke in an odd, yet gentle tone. "You really are an angel."

The vehicle backed into the street, and before Angel could respond, he'd already rounded the corner and was out of sight.

Chapter Fourteen

Angel lifted her face to the sun and let it warm her skin. If she were a cat, she'd have stretched and emitted a loud satisfied purr.

This drug buy had gone without a hitch. Despite his initial reluctance, it hadn't taken Mike long to secure an eight-ball of meth. She couldn't understand why he'd balked when she'd told him she now wanted twice that much, but only if he could get it to her by Friday.

"That's only a couple of days." He'd frowned.

Angel shrugged. "Not my problem. My friends told me they want it by then. If you can't deliver, I'll find someone else who can."

"No. Don't do that." Mike rubbed his hands

together as if warming them over a campfire. "I can get it. But it's going to cost you."

"How much?"

Mike named a figure twice the going rate.

Angel pretended to choke.

He repeated the amount.

Angel had to give the boy credit. He wasn't the slightest bit apologetic. She narrowed her gaze and studied him for a moment. "For a couple of eight-balls? That's way too high."

"Take it or leave it." He leaned back against the concession building that sat to the north of the ball field and folded his arms across his chest. "It's quality stuff."

"There's a lot of good stuff out there." More and more every day, according to the police reports.

"Not for long." Mike shifted. For an instant his confident facade wavered, and she caught a glimpse of fear. "The cops are putting on the heat. A lot of labs are shutting down. For a while, anyway."

Cops putting on the heat? What was the guy talking about? As far as she knew there'd been no change in the department's plan of attack. Unfortunately, even an unsubstantiated rumor held the power to send everyone scurrying underground. If that happened, she was done. The other agencies were already vying to take charge of the investigation, and she needed results.

The funds the department had earmarked for this investigation weren't unlimited, but after a few calculations in her head, Angel concluded there was enough to meet his price.

"I can get the money," she said. "But then I want a lot more of the stuff. Thirty-two grams."

Mike shook his head. "The best I could do would be sixteen."

"Thirty."

"Sixteen," he said firmly, his jaw tightening.

"Twenty-four?" She flashed him an imploring smile. Even though it wasn't her own money, she couldn't let him take advantage of her. Plus, haggling was an expected part of the negotiation process.

Mike heaved an exasperated sigh and stroked his jaw thoughtfully. "Twenty-four."

A sense of triumph swept through her, and she resisted the urge to grin. "By Friday."

"I'll do my best."

"Don't give me that." Angel squinted at him. She had to put the pressure on him to act quickly. "If you can't get me the stuff by then, I need to know."

The *crack* of a bat connecting split the air. Mike

leaned around the edge of the building. Angel did the same.

Without the building in the way, they had a perfect view of the ball field. The reserves were practicing, and Mike was supposed to be helping Jake coach the shortstops.

"I need to get going."

She grabbed his arm just in time. "You'll talk to your contact tonight?"

"Yeah, I'll talk to him—" He stopped as if realizing that in his hurry to get back to practice, he'd gotten sloppy. He'd inadvertently let Angel know his contact was a man.

Jake Weston?

Even though she didn't believe it, the thought made her sick. "Call me tomorrow and let me know for sure."

He gave her a jerky nod, his eyes back on the field, his mind now elsewhere.

She stood and watched him head onto the field. Crow had been right. He'd told her to go for the big buy and force their hand. Even though she couldn't see her partner, she knew he was out there, watching Mike's every move, waiting for the boy to lead him to the main man.

And although Angel knew it was a selfish request, she breathed a silent prayer that Jake wouldn't be that man.

She debated whether or not to hang around and watch practice. Lots of kids did, both girls and guys, but Angel had never been one of them. What would Jake do if he saw her in the stands? Would he come over to talk? Or would the fear of how it would look keep him away?

He seemed to have overcome his original reluctance to be involved with her. That is, if the carnival and a ride home made them "involved." But still he obviously had to keep their relationship private.

If she was honest with herself, Angel had to admit it still bothered her that he'd kissed her. He didn't know she was an adult. To him, she was still a high school senior. She wasn't sure how he'd rationalized his own behavior.

She inhaled a deep breath and released it, determined not to waste another minute of this glorious day worrying about something that in the long run wouldn't matter, anyway. The case would end soon, and she'd never see him again.

Footsteps sounded. *Probably another student coming to watch practice.* Angel turned. A tall bearded man with a scar across his right brow and an ominous glint in his eyes stood behind her. Like a striking snake, one large hand shot out and clamped over her mouth, the other grabbed her arms in a viselike grip.

The smell of male sweat burned her nostrils. Her adrenaline kicked into high gear. She lifted one foot and came down hard on her assailant's instep.

He loosened his hold, and the second her arms were free her elbow shot back and caught him full in the ribs.

The man doubled over, and Angel shoved his head down at the same time she brought her knee up, smashing it into his face. She heard a sickening *crunch*. Blood streamed from his nose.

Angel stepped back, her breath coming hard. Her gaze swept the area and her heart rate skyrocketed. He wasn't alone. Two other men were right behind him!

She did her best—her training officer would have been proud—but the odds were too great. While the tall skinny man held her tight against him, Mr. Broken Nose and the other riffled through her pockets. It didn't take them long to find what they were looking for—a small packet formed out of magazine paper.

"Let's go." A balding guy with bad skin smiled with satisfaction and slipped the packet of crystal meth into his pocket. Angel vaguely remembered him from an aggravated assault case last year.

The guy holding her muttered what sounded like agreement.

Only the mountain of a man with the big hands

who had originally grabbed her seemed unwilling to let her off so easily.

"Not so fast. The little—" He stopped and spat out two teeth. He stared at the ground. A murderous look of fury crossed his face.

Angel took a deep breath. With her arms trapped, this guy would be free to do as he pleased.

He took a step forward. Angel let loose a blood-curdling scream. With each step he took closer, she screamed louder, until his hand clamped around her throat and cut off her air.

She kicked out and fought to breathe.

"What's going on here!" Jake's angry voice sounded behind her.

The men scattered like rats. Angel had a brief view of a few players in pursuit before her legs turned to mush.

"Guys, let 'em go," Jake said.

Jake's arms came around her shoulders, and she leaned against him momentarily, grateful for the support. She took a deep breath and let it out slowly. It could have been so much worse. She'd been lucky. A few more minutes and...

Jake turned to Mike. "Get the police."

Angel stiffened and pushed free of Jake's arms, her heart racing. What if the officers recognized her and blew her cover? "No police." Her gaze darted to Mike, and she shook her head.

Dear God, please. Not when we're so close.

The boy hesitated, shifting from one foot to the other. "Coach, if she doesn't want—"

"I said call them," Jake snapped. "Now."

Mike didn't budge. A worried frown creased his forehead, and Angel knew the robbery hadn't been part of his plan. Obviously Crow wasn't the only one keeping an eye on Mike. The guys that attacked her must have been watching him, too, and decided to pick up some free stuff.

"There's no need to call anyone," Angel said through gritted teeth. She shoved aside her pain and forced a smile. "I'm fine."

"You've just been attacked by three men and you're *fine?*" Jake snorted. "I don't think so."

"I'm fine," she repeated.

The student manager jogged up, his breath coming in short puffs. He spoke to Jake, but his smug gaze was directed to Mike. "I called the police, Coach."

"Thanks, Nathan."

Jake turned to Angel. "I promise. We'll get the guys that did this to you."

"Call them back." Her vocal cords had taken a beating and her voice croaked like a raspy frog. "Tell them not to come. I'm not going to press charges."

"I know the last thing you want to do is talk

about it.'' His voice was as soft and gentle as the breeze. "But it has to be done."

"You don't underst—"

"Don't worry." Jake's hand closed over her shoulder, and he gave it a squeeze. "I'll be here with you."

Angel closed her eyes and said a quick prayer. If ever there was a time she could use some divine intervention, it was now.

"Over here, officers." Nathan held out his arm and cleared a path for the police.

The older officer's gaze scanned the group of players that had stayed behind wanting to be in on the excitement. "You boys can go on home."

They hesitated, talking low amongst themselves.

"Hit the showers," Jake ordered.

Most knew better than to argue with the coach. Like a lumbering herd, they headed for the locker room.

Angel could feel Jake's puzzled gaze, but she kept her eyes focused on the south wall of the concession stand as if she'd never seen peeling paint before.

"You two can go, too." This time it was the older cop who spoke.

Angel slanted a gaze sideways. Mike and Nathan had remained behind.

Jake blew out a frustrated breath. "I thought I told you guys to hit the showers."

Nathan opened his mouth, but Jake didn't give him a chance to protest. "Go."

The boy's face fell, but Angel could tell he was used to following orders. He pushed up his glasses, turned and left without another word. But Mike remained, casting anxious glances at Angel.

"You go on, Mike." Jake smiled reassuringly at the boy. "I'll take care of Angel."

"I can take care of myself." Angel's gaze locked with his.

Jake's lips twitched, and she wondered if he'd said it just to get her attention.

Mike directed one last searching look her way. "Catch ya later?"

She nodded.

He shoved his hands in his pockets and headed up the hill to the school without a backward glance.

Mike had barely disappeared from sight when the younger of the two police officers spoke. With his round baby face and shock of sandy-red hair, he couldn't have been more than thirty. And he looked vaguely familiar. Angel stifled an uneasy feeling.

"I'm Officer Dunlevey, and this is Officer Lee. Why don't you tell us what happened?"

Jake recounted how they'd been practicing and had heard a scream, and then described in detail the scene he'd come upon between the three men and Angel.

Officer Dunlevey wrote down the descriptions of the three and the two cops exchanged knowing glances.

Jake picked up on it immediately. "So, you think you know them?"

"Maybe." Officer Dunlevey was noncommittal. His gaze locked firmly on Angel.

She held her breath. Although she didn't know either of the two officers personally, she'd seen them both around the station.

"I guess I don't understand." The younger officer took a step forward, a puzzled frown on his face. "What are you doing here?"

Angel's heart missed a beat. "Going to high school." She spoke slowly and clearly, her eyes daring him to disagree.

Dunlevey's frown deepened.

"Brian, if you don't mind. I'd like to question the victim." Officer Lee spoke for the first time, and Angel could have kissed him. The seasoned veteran knew something was up, and although he didn't understand it, Angel knew, he wouldn't give her away.

Her tense muscles relaxed even as a surge of

excitement swept through her. This could be the moment of truth. If she played this right—if *they* played this right—she might not only keep her cover, but discover once and for all where Jake Weston stood.

"So, how much did they get?" Officer Lee asked softly, his eyes narrowing. The man was playing his part to perfection.

Jake raised a questioning brow. "What are you talking about?"

"She knows." The older officer glanced down at the report. "Don't you, Angel?"

Jake glanced at her. She refused to meet his eyes, and he found it hard to swallow past the lump in his throat. Still, he had to know. "Can someone please tell me what's going on here?"

The two officers looked at Angel. She stood with her arms crossed, and every curve of her body spoke defiance.

Jake took a deep steadying breath. "Angel?"

She lifted her chin and remained silent.

Dunlevey tapped his pencil against his notepad. "Do you still have any of the stuff on you, *Angel?*"

"Go ahead and search me." Her eyes flashed. "You won't find anything."

The two cops exchanged glances.

"They got it," Dunlevey said with a resigned air that would have seemed theatrical in another setting.

"Hey," Jake said. "She's the victim here. They could have hurt her. They could have *killed* her."

Just the thought made him sick. And the way they were talking about her as if she were some sort of criminal... All of a sudden, his earlier fear that she could be a drug dealer hit him full force. Why had he been so sure she couldn't be involved in such things?

Because you're like your brother. A soft touch. A fool.

Despite the mounting evidence, Jake resisted believing the worst. She could still be undercover, couldn't she?

But if she was a cop, wouldn't these two recognize her? Even if they denied it, Jake should be able to see it in their faces. In a final attempt to prove his worst fears wrong, Jake decided to pull out all the stops.

"Look at her." His voice was insistent. "Doesn't she look familiar?"

Startled, her eyes met his.

Officer Lee's face was expressionless. "Nope, never seen her."

"Angel," Dunlevey repeated, as if testing the

word against his tongue. He stared thoughtfully for a moment.

Angel narrowed her gaze.

Finally the young officer nodded. "I do know her."

Angel's eyes widened. Officer Lee stared at his partner as if he'd never seen him before.

Jake breathed a prayer of thanks.

"I busted her once in East St. Louis."

Horrified, Jake looked up.

The officer shook his head, and the last of Jake's hope died with his words. "Another dope deal gone bad. And this little Angel was right in the middle of it."

"Angel?"

Her heart clenched at the look of pain on Jake's face. She knew he wanted her to deny it, but how could she when it was all true?

She turned her attention to the young officer. She now realized why Dunlevey looked so familiar. It was only now that she made the connection.

Ten years ago he'd been a rookie, more a boy than a man, working some of the roughest streets in the country. That hot sticky July night, he'd come with another officer in response to the report of shots being fired.

Between the lights, the sirens and the crowd of

rowdy bystanders, that dingy street corner had taken on a surreal, almost circus-like atmosphere. Her uncle only added to the picture. The man had been out of control, spitting and cursing and, when that didn't work, screaming police brutality. High on crank, his focus was on everyone but his niece—a fifteen-year-old girl crumpled on a dirty sidewalk in a pool of blood.

The bullet had nicked an artery, and as one of the first responders, it had been Officer Dunlevey's assignment to keep pressure on the wound until the paramedics arrived.

Now she stared solemnly at the officer. "I never said thank you."

A look of surprise flashed across his features. "I was only doing my job."

"You saved my life," she said softly.

"So, it's true." Jake's voice was heavy with disappointment.

Angel dropped her gaze and kicked the dirt with the toe of her sneaker. One of her clips had come loose, and she pushed back her hair with a surprisingly shaky hand. A return to that time, even if only in her memory, did not come without cost. "Yes, it's true."

The officers suddenly seemed anxious to wrap up their investigation. They asked a few more cursory questions and left.

Jake let out a pent-up breath. "I'll take you home."

The offer was grudging, but to Angel, the thought of walking held no appeal. "Thanks."

They headed to the Jeep in an uneasy silence. Angel wasn't sure what hurt more, her bruised neck or the knowledge she'd disappointed him.

When she'd accepted this assignment, all she'd thought about was the good she'd be doing: getting drugs off the street and out of the hands of kids. She'd never once considered that her deception would cause pain to someone she cared about.

The ten-minute ride home seemed like an eternity. Angel, who rarely found herself at a loss for words, didn't know what to say. She couldn't explain without blowing her cover, and wasting her breath insisting she wasn't a drug dealer would be pointless in light of the evidence against her.

She should have felt relieved when he pulled in front of her house. Instead, the knowledge that the closeness they'd shared was gone twisted like a knife inside her.

If only she could know for sure where he stood. She'd always relied on her gut instincts, and her gut was 99.9-percent certain he was exactly as he appeared. But it was that one-tenth of one percent doubt that gave her pause. How could she risk the entire operation for the sake of her heart?

He turned off the motor and leaned his head back against the seat, lines of fatigue edging his mouth.

She was acutely aware of his presence, the warmth radiating from his body, the spicy scent of his cologne, his handsome profile that now looked set in stone.

Tentatively she reached out to touch his arm. "None of this has anything to do with the way I feel about you."

He jerked away and his eyes blazed hot with anger. "How can you say that? You're a liar. A fraud."

Angel stared at him in astonishment. "Jake, can't you understand—"

"Understand?" His voice dripped with sarcasm. "What? That you want to sell drugs to kids? That it doesn't affect us because it's just business? No, I can't understand that. My whole life is focused on helping these kids, not ruining their lives."

Harsh and blunt though they were, his words gave her hope. Unless Jake was the best actor she'd ever seen, he *was* the man she'd thought him to be.

"Jake…"

"Angel—" He reached across her and opened the door. "Go. Please."

She stared at the face of this man she loved.

Loved? Even though she tried to deny it, she knew it was true. And she wasn't going to wait until it was too late to say it. "I love you."

His expression hardened. "Love?" he said derisively. "You don't know what love is. Love isn't coming on to every man you meet."

She paused. Granted, she might have come on a little strong, but that had been an act, all part of the investigation. "I have never—"

"Don't give me that." He cut her off without apology. "I can think of four guys off the top of my head—" Jake held up his hand and counted them off. "Crow. Then there's Mike, your best friend's guy, but why let that stop you?"

"Will you just listen to me!"

He shook his head and continued. "Then there's Jarvis. What was it you said to him at the Bible study? Something about how you liked to party and there was no need to worry about telling the boyfriend?"

"You misunderstood—"

"Let me finish." He pressed his lips together for a second. "And, of course, there's Jake Weston, the biggest fool of them all."

A look of pain crossed his face, and a band tightened around her heart. She started to speak, but again he cut her off.

"Four men in three months. Quite a record."

"You can't believe that." Hot tears stung the back of her eyes. "You can't think that I did anything with those guys."

"You came on to me. You let me kiss you," he said. "And I probably could have done a lot more than just kiss you if I had wanted. And *I* was your teacher."

Anger surged. Her head pounded and her cheeks burned as if they were on fire. She wasn't sure what bothered her more—that he'd accused her of being promiscuous or that he'd brought out into the open the one flaw in his character that she kept shoving to the side.

"Let's talk about that, shall we?" Her gaze met his without flinching, any hint of tears gone. "You're a *teacher*. I'm a *student*. What kind of man kisses a *child?*"

His face flushed, and he sputtered, "Are you calling me—"

Angel interrupted him with the same lack of regard he'd shown her. "If the shoe fits—"

"Let me tell you, Angel Morelli, I never would have kissed you if I hadn't known—"

The ringing of her cell phone stopped his words. She answered it immediately. Only Crow had this number, and it was to be used only in emergencies. "This is Angel."

"We need to talk." Crow's voice was tight and controlled.

"Hold on." She looked at Jake. "It's one of my many lovers. He needs me desperately."

She pushed the door fully open and slid out, casting Jake one last glance. "I'm sure you understand such desires."

The door slammed shut. On their relationship. And on her heart.

"Go ahead," she said in a seductive voice loud enough for Jake to hear. "I'm all yours, babe."

Chapter Fifteen

Tom Jorgen's sprawling ranch sat on approximately five acres outside Woodland Hills in an affluent subdivision known as Echo Park. The area was heavily wooded, and Angel had carefully hidden her car in some overgrown brush down the road.

She'd come immediately in response to her partner's call. Even with his directions, it had taken her a while to find him. He sat in the shadows of the trees edging Tom's property, his high-power binoculars specially made for night viewing in his lap.

"How long has Mike been in there?"

"Over an hour. He came here right from the ball field."

Angel frowned. "Where's his car?"

"Must be at home with his other toys. This time he came on a Harley. One of those old ones, an Indian, I think." Crow shook his head in amazement.

Angel wasn't into motorcycles at all, but it was apparent Crow was impressed. "Where is it?"

"In the garage," Crow said. "The kid drove up like he owned the place. He punched a remote and he was in."

Angel's brows knit together. "So, he comes here a lot."

"Looks like it." Crow glanced at her sideways. "By the way, how are you doing? Those were some mean dudes."

"I'm okay," she lied. She wasn't fine at all. Her head ached, her neck ached, and most of all her heart ached. "That big guy was something else."

"Good thing Weston showed up."

"Yeah, I guess." Angel didn't want to talk about Jake. It had been a long time since she'd been so disappointed.

"Speaking of Weston—" Crow jerked his head in the direction of the drive "—look who's decided to join the party."

Angel turned her head slowly and her heart sank at the sight of the Jeep pulling up to the house. "What's he doing here?"

Although Crow's poker face gave little away, for an instant Angel swore his disappointment mirrored hers. But Angel knew she must have been mistaken—Crow had never liked Jake.

"My guess is—joining his partners," he responded.

Shocked, she could only stare. "You actually think—"

"He's one of them." Crow draped his arm companionably around Angel's shoulder. "Good thing we never let him in on the investigation."

Crow was being kind when he said "we." *She'd* been the one convinced all along of Jake's innocence.

"Yeah." She remembered how close she'd come to confiding in Jake. "It's a real good thing."

Tom Jorgens leaned back in his leather wingback chair, his fingers steepled beneath his chin. "By Friday."

Mike nodded. "I know you said you wanted to back off for a while, but I thought maybe one last time...."

"I don't know." It wasn't like Tom to be so indecisive, but he really *didn't* know. His sources were usually reliable and they'd warned him to be extra careful. "Any chance that girl's a cop?"

"Angel?" Mike laughed. "No way."

Irritated by the boy's cavalier attitude toward something so serious, Tom's voice came out harsher than he intended. "How can you be so sure?"

"For one, she's just a girl. She's not old enough to be a cop," Mike said confidently. "For another, I recognized those guys that stole her stuff. If she was a cop, they would have known her. Third, she didn't tell the cops any—"

"That's enough." Tom waved him silent, tired of the boy's ramblings. He supposed it wouldn't hurt to get rid of some of the extra stuff he had on hand. Just in case.

Still, in some ways he'd like to keep it for himself. It was surprising how he'd grown to view snorting the meth as a way of life. And even though he'd made the decision to save it for "special occasions," a part of him resisted limiting the one thing that brought him pleasure.

"Hey, man. I don't have all night. What'll it be? Yes or no?" Mike spoke with the impatience reserved for the young.

Tom rose and paced the room. He had a bad feeling about this whole deal, but he couldn't put his finger on why.

"They'll be paying top dollar," Mike said, as if that would be an added incentive.

"The money doesn't matter," Tom said.

"Don't give me that, man." The teen laughed. "As much as you do, you couldn't afford not to sell."

"You think you know so much." Tom shook his head in disgust. "You don't know anything."

Getting involved in the manufacturing and sale of the stuff had never been about the money. Initially it was a way to have a guaranteed supply. Then it had been about the thrill—the rush of feeling alive again, of living on the edge. It had been about the forgetting. When he was high on crystal he didn't think about Jane, and he didn't miss her quite so much.

Tom glanced at the boy. It wasn't about money for Mike, either. The kid's folks were loaded, and he had access to unlimited funds. And Mike didn't even like to use that much. "It's not about the money for you, either, is it?"

Mike shifted and stared Tom straight in the eye. "If I wanted to talk about my feelings, I'd see a shrink."

Tom nodded approvingly. There was nothing soft and wimpy about this kid. He realized suddenly he liked Mike, liked his in-your-face attitude. "Okay, we'll do it. One last time. You'll have your stuff by Friday."

"Is Gade closed down for good, then?"

Tom nodded. It had been a difficult decision to abandon the meth lab they had over in Trashtown. But when he'd found out it was under surveillance, he'd had no choice. "It's gone."

"You're making the stuff here?" Mike's voice was incredulous.

He could understand the boy's surprise. Although he'd had the lab set up in the laundry room area off the garage for some time, they'd rarely used it. For no particular reason other than that he felt uncomfortable doing something he knew Jane would not approve of in what had been her house.

"I don't have much choice," Tom said dryly. "Right now, it's all we have."

"At least you're out in the sticks." Mike wrinkled his nose. "Nobody should complain about the smell."

That had been the problem on Gade. Some of the neighbors had noticed a strange lingering odor and reported it.

"That's where living in 'the sticks' has its advantages," Tom said wryly, wondering what his neighbors would think of hearing their exclusive area referred to in such a manner.

"I need to get going." Mike rose just as the doorbell rang.

The two exchanged worried glances. Tom

waved Mike back down and headed for the door. "I'll get rid of them."

Jake shifted uneasily on Tom's front step and hit the doorbell again. He sniffed. A strange odor that reminded him of shoe polish hung in the air. He sniffed again and hoped Tom didn't take too long to answer the door. The smell was giving him a headache.

He glanced around the porch. He hadn't been to the house since Jane's funeral, and then the air had been filled with the cloying scent of flowers reserved for the dead.

He pushed the memory aside and focused on his reason for being here, although he still wasn't sure he should have come. On the one hand, Tom had a right to know what was going on in his school. On the other hand, Jake couldn't help but feel disloyal to Angel.

The thought that he could still feel anything for her after what she'd done showed just how big a fool he was. Jake raised his hand, ready to punch the bell one more time. Without warning, the door swung partially open.

"Jake." Tom's eyes widened. "What are you doing here?"

"I need to talk to you." Jake hesitated, surprised

when Tom didn't immediately open the door and invite him in. "It's important."

Still, the principal hesitated.

"What's it about?" Tom's gaze narrowed. "Couldn't it wait?"

"Actually it can't," Jake said. "It's about Angel Morelli, one of the students that transferred in this semester. I found out something from the cops that I think you should know."

He'd finally gotten the man's attention. Tom opened the door wider and motioned Jake inside.

"Thanks, Tom. I—" Jake stopped short.

Mike Blaine stood in the foyer, clearly on his way out. "Mr. Jorgens, thanks for taking the time to talk to me. I appreciate it."

Tom's face was inscrutable. "Anytime, Mike."

Mike shot Jake a hurried smile. "Coach."

Jake nodded. "Mike."

The door slammed shut behind the boy.

Thoroughly puzzled, Jake turned to Tom. "What was he doing here?"

Tom hesitated. "I really can't say too much other than the boy has some personal issues I'm helping him with."

"Why you?" Jake asked bluntly.

Tom raised an eyebrow. "In case you've forgotten—" Tom spaced his words and spoke distinctly, his irritation at being questioned evident "—I have a masters degree in counseling."

Actually, Jake *had* forgotten. "That's right. You were a chemistry teacher, got the masters in counseling and in—"

"—educational administration." Tom filled in the blank and motioned Jake into the kitchen. "Now tell me about this Angel person."

There was the distinctive rumble of a Harley-Davidson starting up, followed by a backfire. Tom paled. "The fool—"

An explosion rocked the house and the windows shattered.

For a frightening instant time stood still. Angel had heard of this happening. It wasn't at all unusual. After all, some of the ingredients used in making crystal were highly volatile, and any little spark could cause the lab to blow.

"Tell 'em we need an ambulance and let 'em know it was a meth lab that blew!" Crow yelled.

Angel punched in the numbers, relayed the message, then took off running toward the house. Toward Jake.

Chapter Sixteen

"The doctors said you were all very lucky." Nancy Weston handed Jake a cup of hot cocoa. She set a plate of cookies on the table before taking a seat opposite him.

He took a sip to humor her, then put the mug on the place mat in front of him. "Is that what they said?"

Lucky? Funny, he didn't feel lucky. Oh, he knew it had been a miracle the three of them had survived with such minor injuries. Mike had been hurt the worst, but less than two weeks later his burns had already started to heal. But all Jake felt now was tired. And disappointed.

"When I think I could have lost you, too..."

His mother's hands trembled and her cup joined his on the table.

"Well, you didn't." Jake reached over and covered her hand with his. Sometimes it was easy to forget how hard this had been on her. "And now that they finally believe I wasn't involved, it looks like I won't be taking that trip down the road to the state penitentiary."

"That was the most ridiculous thing I'd ever heard." Her eyes flashed, and Jake realized the formidableness of a mother's ire. "I told that detective my son would never be involved in making or selling drugs. The very idea."

"I told them, too," Jake said, remembering the endless interrogation. The one thing that had surprised him was that no one seemed interested in Angel and Crow's involvement. When he'd mentioned they'd been there that night, the cops had taken down their names, but their questions had revolved around Tom and Mike and what Jake knew about them.

Out of curiosity, he'd checked with the school once he'd left the hospital to see if Angel was still attending classes. He wasn't surprised to learn she'd transferred out of the district.

Yeah, right.

"What do you think made them finally believe you?"

Jake shook his head, then winced. He'd sustained a concussion in the explosion, and his head still hurt. "I'm not sure. I know Tom tried to say it was just him, but they had some other evidence against Mike."

"That's too bad about the boy. And about Mr. Jorgens. He always seemed like such a nice man."

Just thinking of the charges the two of them faced made Jake sick. They'd both had so much going for them. "Tom was a good guy. But when Jane died, he just fell apart."

"I think it'd be easy to do without faith." His mother's gaze dropped to the table as if the green gingham place mats she'd given him last Christmas were fascinating. "There were times after Jim's death when I wondered if I could go on, but thankfully God was with me every step of the way."

"I still miss him," Jake said.

She looked up, and a deep sadness reflected back at him. "I do, too."

They sat in silence, drinking the hot cocoa, until his mother spoke again. "Did I tell you I got a letter from Anton and Carlos?"

"I didn't know you corresponded with them." He might have forgiven them, but there was no way he wanted to be a part of their lives. Actually, he was surprised his mother did.

"We don't *correspond*." His mother emphasized the word. "I had sent them a note after they were sentenced, and Carlos wrote once."

"How nice." Jake raised the cup to his lips.

"They'd received your letter."

He took a sip. "Did they?"

"It meant a lot to them to have your forgiveness."

"Something needed but not deserved," he murmured, remembering Angel's words.

His mother frowned and set her cup down again. "What did you say?"

Jake shook his head. "Nothing. I was just remembering something a friend had said."

His mother's eyes widened and her hand rose to her chest. "I can't believe I forgot. Your friend dropped by."

His heart lodged in his throat, and Angel's image flashed before him. Until he remembered she was long gone. "Who was it?"

"Amanda Delahay. She stopped by while you were sleeping. I told her I'd wake you up, but she wouldn't hear of it. She said to just tell you she hoped you'd be feeling better soon."

Jake frowned. "I wonder why she didn't want to stay."

"I think I know why." His mother's eyes twinkled. "I glanced out the window when she left. There was a man waiting out in the car for her."

"Amanda's got a boyfriend?" Jake's brow creased. Why did he find that so hard to believe? She was a beautiful woman with a lot of good qualities. Just because she'd never been right for him didn't mean she wouldn't be perfect for someone else.

"Oh, honey, I'm sorry. You'd told me you and she weren't dating anymore." She cast him a concerned glance. "I assumed you were over her. I should have known you'd still have some feelings for—"

He placed his hand over hers. "I don't have any feelings for her. None at all."

"Are you sure?"

"Positive," he said. "She and I had a long talk a couple of weeks ago. It never would have worked. We wanted different things in life. The funny thing was, I wasn't even her first choice. She admitted something I'd suspected all along—she'd been more interested in Jim than me."

"Your brother?" Her hand jerked back; she looked as though she'd been struck. "I don't know what she said but I know my Jim. He would never have gone after your girl—"

"Relax, Mom." Jake smiled. "She was the one who did the pursuing. He turned her down flat."

"Good for Jim." She nodded approvingly.

"And you don't want any woman who thinks you're second best. You have a lot to offer."

"Thanks for the vote of confidence." He wanted to chuckle, but she was so serious he didn't dare.

"What about your new girlfriend? The dark-haired one?"

"She's long gone." The knowledge that she was indeed long gone brought out the sharpness in Jake's tone.

"I wouldn't say *long* gone." His mother snapped a cookie in half and took a bite. "She was at the hospital."

"You met her?" Angel was at the hospital? His mind raced. It hardly seemed possible. Why would she have come there? She had to know the place would be crawling with cops.

Nancy Weston shook her head. "No, I just saw her from a distance."

He blew out the breath he'd been holding, not sure why he felt so disappointed. "It was probably just someone that worked in the hospital."

"I don't think so." His mother's brows drew together in concentration. "Apparently she'd ridden in the ambulance with you. I heard someone say you must have done something right to have an angel at your side."

Angel.

"What do you suppose they meant by that?"

"I have no idea." Jake shrugged and grabbed another cookie. He pasted what he hoped was a uninterested look on his face and kept his voice offhand. "Why didn't you tell me this before?"

"I thought you knew." She smiled sheepishly. "You were holding her hand like she was your lifeline."

Jake groaned to himself, wondering what else he might have done or said.

"It was so sweet." The curiosity in his mother's expression was the last thing he needed to see. "I wanted to ask you about her, but after what you'd said to me about my meddling, I didn't know quite how to bring it up."

"Until now."

"I kept expecting her to stop by. But she never did." His mother dropped the rest of the cookie to the plate. "You should have seen the look on her face in that emergency room, Jake. She wouldn't leave your side."

"I'm surprised they let her stay."

"She wouldn't take no for an answer." His mother paused thoughtfully. "Not even from the police."

Jake didn't know what to say. He didn't want to think about Angel and he certainly didn't want to talk about her. Because he didn't want to miss her, not anymore. He just wanted to forget.

He managed to make small talk for a few more minutes. If only his father wasn't out of town on business. His mother had no reason to hurry home, and Jake couldn't bring himself to tell her he'd rather be alone.

They'd finally decided to rent a movie, when the phone rang. His mother jumped up to answer it.

"Tell them I'm asleep." He had no idea who it could be but he was all talked out. Over the past two weeks, practically the whole school had stopped by or called.

"Weston residence."

Jake hid a grin. His mother never could answer the phone with a simple hello.

A puzzled expression replaced his mother's smile. "Yes, he's here. Can you hold for a minute? I'll get him."

She covered the receiver with her hand. "It's someone named Tony D'Fusco. He's calling from Rome."

"What are you telling me?" Angel sat up straight in her desk chair and stared at Crow. She'd been back at work for over a week, but this was the first time she and her former partner had been able to get together and talk.

He was getting set to go undercover again, and

she knew it would be a long time before she'd see him.

"I'm saying—" Crow leaned back in the chair as if testing how far it could bend without breaking "—that the investigation is closed. Looks like that Mike kid might be able to go into a diversion program. What'll happen to the principal is anyone's guess. It'll help that he wasn't involved in any big-time distribution."

"I can't believe there never was a meth ring," Angel muttered. Their faces had all been red when they'd discovered, after all was said and done, not only that this wasn't an interstate operation, but that it wasn't even an *in-state* one. Actually, they'd explained to the chief, it looked more like a one-man production.

Their superior had complained loud and long about misinformed informants and the cost to the budget, before commending them on a job well done.

"I know," Crow said. "What a bummer. Now this next one is supposed to be big. Sure you won't join me? We made a great team."

"I'm going to have to pass." Angel shook her head. She'd prayed all weekend and now was completely at peace with her decision to go back to her desk job. She'd make her difference in a more traditional way.

"Aren't you going to ask about the boyfriend?"

Angel took a deep breath and smiled as if it didn't matter to her what happened to Jake Weston. In truth, she was dying to know the outcome of the investigation. "You're referring, I take it, to Jake?"

"You bet." Crow's eyes gleamed. "I got the final word today from one of the detectives."

"Go ahead and tell me." She forced a bored-sounding sigh. "I know you're dying to say 'I told you so.'"

"No, babe. I'm the one that owes you an apology." Crow chuckled. "You were right all along."

A tightness in her chest made it difficult to breathe. "He's been cleared? Completely?"

"That's what I'm saying." Crow's eyes gleamed. "He's all yours. Free and clear."

"'Fraid not." Angel wiped a smudge off her desktop with her shirtsleeve. "I'm not his type. Too wild."

"Wild?" Crow hooted. "You're about as straight as they come."

"I think," she said dryly, "he confused the undercover Angel with the real me."

"That's easy enough to take care of." Crow reached for the phone. "Call and set him straight. Or better yet, I'll call him."

"Oh, no you don't." She yanked the phone from his grasp. "If anyone calls him, it'll be me."

But in the end, no one called.

Chapter Seventeen

Jake ran his finger along the collar of his starched white shirt and shifted uncomfortably in the padded chair. He glanced around the crowded auditorium. The evening's event had been planned to highlight citizens who'd made a difference in the lives of the community's youth.

"I didn't expect so many to show up, did you?" Barely above a whisper, his mother's voice still carried to his father sitting on the other side of Jake.

"Jim's not the only one being honored today." His father gestured toward the program brochure in his lap. "There's also a nurse, a social worker and a police officer."

Jake cast a sideways glance at his father. He

noticed the lines of strain around the older man's mouth. A handsome man in his early fifties, John Weston had brown hair now touched with gray, and the perpetual smile that had always hovered on his lips didn't flash readily anymore.

To his right, his mother fidgeted with her purse, her eyes a shade too bright. Coming to this city-wide awards ceremony had been difficult on all of them. Receiving the Educator's Award for Service to Area Youth was an honor his brother well deserved. But he couldn't help wishing Jim could be here to accept the award. It seemed like yesterday that they'd celebrated Jim's graduation from college.

And now he's dead.

The pain of Jim's death would never ease entirely, but at last Jake had come to terms with it. His brother had done a lot of good in his short life. Today was a day to celebrate, not mourn.

"Look—" his mother pointed to the front. "That's Adam Brown, the one that nominated Jim for the award. He was one of your brother's students."

Jake peered at the stage. A young black man, clearly uncomfortable in a shiny blue suit, stood off to the side, shifting from one foot to the other as the master of ceremonies tapped the microphone.

The boy's introduction focused on his background. Raised in a single-parent home, he was now the first in his family to graduate from high school. And thanks to Jim's encouragement and scholarship contacts, he would now be the first to attend college.

Jake folded his hands and listened intently. By the time Adam finished, Jake had a lump in his throat, his mother's eyes were misty, and a muscle twitched in his father's jaw.

"I just want to say one final thing. I've talked a lot about how Mr. Weston helped me academically. But what he did for me went far beyond the classroom. He encouraged me to be the best I could be in all areas of my life. I learned from him what being a man really means and the importance of standing up for what you believe. I learned firsthand what it means to live your faith. And I also learned one of the most important lessons of all—when to shut up. Thank you." The boy's serious expression eased, and he smiled for the first time.

Thunderous applause followed, and Jake's father made his way down the aisle to the podium to accept the award on behalf of his son.

His father returned to his seat with a plaque and a proud smile on his face. Jake took it from his hands, read the inscription, then passed it to his mother. Tears welled in her eyes, and she hugged it to her chest.

He and his father exchanged an understanding smile. Jake took a deep breath and exhaled slowly.

The social worker was honored next, then the nurse. Jake listened with half an ear, unable to keep his thoughts from straying back to his conversation with Tony D'Fusco.

When the guy had confirmed Angel was not only his cousin but a cop as well, Jake hadn't been surprised. Deep down, he'd known she couldn't be involved in drug dealing. Why had he let his foolish pride goad him into saying things he now would give anything to take back?

He'd picked up the phone to call her dozens of times this past week, only to set it back on its cradle without punching a single number. What would he say? *I'm a fool? Please forgive me?*

Yes, a voice inside whispered, *that's exactly what you could say.*

"Jake." His mother's elbow jabbed him square in the ribs. He jerked. "Isn't that your 'friend' on the stage?"

His gaze shot to the dais. There, resplendent in full dress uniform, stood Officer Angel Morelli. His breath caught in his throat.

She moved confidently to the podium. Jake barely heard her acceptance speech. All he could do was stare and think how different things might have been if he'd only trusted his feelings.

A knot formed in the pit of his stomach. He'd been so hung up on being played for a fool that he'd ended up being just that. Angel was everything he'd ever wanted.

Jake leaned forward, his gaze riveted to her.

I'm sorry. He offered up the apology, sending it silently across the space between them, smiling with relief when his eyes met hers and she faltered over her words.

Saying he was sorry didn't make up for the wrong he'd done her, but at least he'd finally said it. And maybe one day she'd forgive him.

Needed, but not deserved.

He shook his head, a wry smile twisting his lips.

"Jake." His father touched his arm. "The program's over. We need to head to the reception area."

"Why don't you ask your friend to join us?" His mother offered a hopeful smile. "I could save a table."

"I don't know, Mom." Jake rose and followed them down the aisle, out of the auditorium and into the huge ballroom. He looked at the cluster of uniformed officers in one corner. "All her friends are here. I'm sure she'll be busy."

"Couldn't you at least bring her over so I could

meet her?'' His mother's face was serious. "I want to thank her for taking such good care of you.''

Jake paused.

"I promise not to ask her any questions,'' she said quickly. "I'll behave myself.''

"Nancy.'' His father shook his head warningly. "Leave the boy alone. When he wants us to meet her, we will.''

"John, you don't understand. Jake already told me he wouldn't introduce me to any woman unless it was the one he planned to marry,'' Nancy said. "I just want him to know I'm not holding him to that ridiculous condition.''

His father and Jake exchanged amused glances. They both knew she could promise all she wanted, but with Nancy Weston, meddling was second nature. There could be no guarantees.

"Honey, I believe I see Jim's old principal over there.'' John cupped his wife's elbow in his hand and gave Jake a wink. "Let's go and say hello.''

His mother protested, but his father paid no attention. Jake watched them maneuver their way through the endless expanse of people. His father's arm reached protectively around his mother's shoulder as the crowd thickened. Jake smiled and turned away.

Despite the fact that he had no intention of interrupting Angel's celebration, he couldn't keep his gaze from straying to the group of cops.

"You're all better." A soft voice sounded behind him.

He whirled. "Angel, hello. Congratulations."

"Thanks." A flush stained her cheeks. "I'm not much for these kinds of things. There are other people who are really much more de—"

"Don't sell yourself short." Even with the brief description during her introduction, Jake could tell the successful program she'd developed for at-risk youth had taken a tremendous amount of time and effort. "You deserved that award."

"Thank you." Clearly embarrassed, she brushed her hair back from her face and smiled.

An awkward silence descended, but she made no move to leave. Jake cleared his throat and for a moment he allowed himself to hope. "I'm sorry for the horrible things I said to you."

"I lied to you," she said simply. "You didn't know if I was a drug dealer or not."

"I'm still sorry."

"Well, since we're talking forgiveness, I want to say I'm sorry, too."

His brow furrowed. "What do you have to be sorry for?"

"For thinking badly of you. For what I said." She took a deep breath. "I talked to my cousin.

He said you two had talked recently, but that you'd been trying to reach him for weeks." She looked him in the eye. "You knew all along I wasn't a student."

He shrugged. "I looked through your backpack that time you left it in the hall. The minute I saw that picture of you and Tony, I knew."

"Why didn't you tell me?"

"I couldn't. For the same reason you couldn't be honest with me."

She gave an embarrassed laugh, and looked down at her hands. "We make quite a pair, don't we?"

"I thought we made a great pair." He cast his pride aside, determined to be honest. "You challenged me, made me understand what grace was all about, and for the first time in almost a year, I felt alive again. No one ever touched a part of my soul like you did."

He shoved his hands in his pockets and rocked back on his heels. "I've missed you, Angel."

She hesitated, but her gaze was strong and steady. "Me, too."

"I'd like to introduce you to my parents."

She tilted her head and studied him for a moment.

"I think you need to know something." His pulses pounded and his palms went damp. "I've told my mother the next woman I introduce to her is the one I plan to marry.''

Her brows pulled together and confusion clouded her gaze.

Jake swallowed hard and plunged ahead. ''I love you, Angel.'' His gaze held hers. ''I want to marry you.''

A stunned look crossed her face, and the small flame of hope that had started to burn inside him flickered. He and Angel had grown close over the past months, but now he couldn't tell what she was thinking. They were meant for each other—deep down, he'd known that from the moment they'd met. If he'd moved too fast, it was only because he was eager to make her his.

A smile tugged at her lips, and the flame of hope began to burn anew in him.

''Are you sure you want to marry someone who looks like she could be your student?'' She twisted a strand of hair around her finger and regarded him with an expression that was so mischievous he had to laugh.

''If you're sure you can marry someone who looks old enough to be your teacher.''

She raised a finger to her lips and pretended to think. ''Well...''

''How 'bout if I throw in a Hawaii honeymoon as an extra incentive? Think of it...lounging on the beach, the sand between your toes, the smell of the salty breeze?''

"I never should have let you in on that secret.'' She heaved an exaggerated sigh and pretended to be irritated, but she couldn't quite carry it off. Not with her smile widening every moment. "Okay. I'll marry you.''

He pulled her into his arms and kissed her soundly—grateful he no longer needed to keep his love undercover. From his friends. Or from his family.

Jake opened his eyes to find his mother standing behind Angel, staring unabashedly, a delighted smile spreading across her face.

He turned his soon-to-be wife in his arms. "Mom, I'd like you to meet Angel Morelli. She's agreed to marry me—'' he shot Angel a smile "—in exchange for a Hawaii honeymoon.''

"I knew it.'' Nancy Weston turned to her husband. Triumph rang in her voice. "Didn't I tell you, John?''

Puzzled, Jake frowned. "What are you talking about?''

His father heaved a long-suffering sigh and shot Jake an apologetic look. "Your mother is thrilled because it looks like she's not going to have to cancel the reservations at the church, after all.''

Jake groaned. "Tell me you didn't reserve the church for June?"

"It's impossible to get at the last minute." His mother's chin lifted. "And June is a beautiful month for a wedding."

Angel's eyes twinkled. "I'd have to agree."

"I like her, Jake." Nancy Weston nodded approvingly.

His father shook his head. "Son, I can see it now. They'll be a formidable twosome. Sure you can handle them?"

"Handle them?" Jake smiled wickedly at Angel. "I can hardly wait."

* * * * *

Dear Reader,

Every day the media bombards us with stories of senseless tragedies, innocent lives lost as a result of the actions of drunk drivers or violent criminals.

I look at my family and wonder what I would do if they were ever the victims of such crimes.

Like Jake Weston, I know I would struggle to make sense of something that would make no sense. And I, too, would find it incredibly hard to forgive.

But yet I know I daily sin and God freely gives me his grace. How could I do any less?

I pray that when you and I are faced with difficult situations, we will draw on God's strength to sustain us and remember His mercy.

Cynthia Rutledge